IVAN SOUTHALL

Benson Boy

Pictures by Ingrid Fetz

THE MACMILLAN COMPANY
New York, New York

Benson Boy was published under the title *Over the Top* by Methuen Children's Books Ltd. in Great Britain in 1972 and simultaneously in Australia by Hicks Smith & Sons Pty. Ltd.

Text Copyright © 1972 Ivan Southall
Copyright © 1973 The Macmillan Company
The Macmillan Company, 866 Third Avenue, New York, N.Y. 10022
Library of Congress catalog card number: 72-81058
Printed in the United States of America

10   9   8   7   6   5   4   3   2   1

Library of Congress Cataloging in Publication Data

Southall, Ivan.
   Benson boy.

   SUMMARY: With his mother about to give birth and his father unconscious from a fall, it's up to eleven-year-old Perry to take charge.
   First published in 1972 under title: Over the top.
   [1. Family life—Fiction]   I. Fetz, Ingrid, illus.   II. Title.
PZ7.S726Be   [Fic]   72-81058   ISBN 0-02-786070-1

Benson
Boy

Contents

1
Stepping Off
the Edge

Perry was wide-eyed awake in the deep darkness, suddenly sitting up in bed and wondering why, trying to grope back into the dream or whatever it might have been that had snapped him out of sleep yet left him so confused. Had someone called his name?

A cold wind was slapping at the window blind three or four feet from his head and steady rain was murmuring on the roof. Dad had been hoping for rain. Dad had been saying, "It had better rain soon." As if he might do something drastic if it didn't. "I'll put a bomb under the Weather Bureau," Dad had been saying. "That'll cook their little goose." Had *that* made it rain?

Sitting there, swaying, trying to work it all out was

like coming without warning upon a strange place a long way from home. There was a gap in Perry's world and it lay between bedtime and getting up again. The middle of the night was an alien world he had not explored. Lots of stories he had heard, lots of tales, lots of rumors about what happened there. Murders and storms and robbers and ogres, there wasn't much he had missed, but never had he been in it wide awake before.

Something was happening.

There were thuds and voices and a flickering yellow glow casting strange-looking shadows on Perry's door where it stood open against the wall, shadows that might have been Dad in the passage outside reaching with a match to light the lamp. *Or* was the house burning down?

"Da-a-ad. Is that you?"

"Yes, Perry."

It was good to know that, mighty good to be sure, even though Dad sounded different and Mum, for some reason to be explained, seemed to be thudding round like an elephant in the next bedroom.

"What are you doing, Dad?"

A second match struck and Dad with a hand cupped about the flame came in and swooped on the window to shut it with a thud, to shut out the cold. Dad had a wild and woolly look about him, half in his pajamas and half out of them, with hair standing stiffly on end as it often was first thing in the morning until he slicked it down. "I want you to dress, Perry."

Dad sounded breathless as if he had run half a mile and the flame in his hand dropped to Perry's bedside candle and settled there, flaring, lighting up his face so that it hung in the dark almost like a mask with a light inside it, troubling Perry.

"What is it, Dad? What's wrong? What are you looking like that for?"

"Nothing's wrong, but I want you to dress as quickly as you can."

"Is the house burning down?"

Dad's smile was short, almost impatient, as if he wished to hurry away. "Would I be lighting candles?"

"Well, what have I got to get dressed for?"

"We can't leave you here, can we? You wouldn't thank us if you woke in the morning and found the house empty, would you? It's just that it's caught us by surprise. There's nowhere else you can go."

"But I don't want to go anywhere."

"Perry, we're off to hospital with your mother. That's why you were called."

"Going *now*?"

"That's what I said."

"Going *now*? In the middle of the night? Can't she wait till the morning?"

"No, she can't. When babies are ready to be born they're ready to be born. You don't start arguing about it."

"Well, you ought to." Perry felt very cross. It was *ridiculous*. "You ought to tell that baby to wait till the morning. The way you'd tell me. I thought it wasn't coming until next week."

"It's changed its mind and it's coming now."

"That stupid baby," Perry wailed. "Is that the sort of baby we're going to have? One that won't wait till the morning when it ought to wait till next week? One that gets me out of bed when it's cold? It's raining out there; haven't you noticed? You'd better put your foot down, Dad. You tell them we don't want that baby. We'll have another one."

But Dad hadn't stopped to listen.

"I don't want to get up."

But Dad had nothing more to say. People were always doing that to Perry. Cutting out in the middle when he was talking to them. So he banged his head on the pillow and dragged the sheet over his face, grumbling to himself, then sharply sat up again. "What time is it?" he bellowed.

A sigh was audible from the other side of the wall. "Ten past two."

"*Ten past two*! Gee, Dad, that's terrible. Getting a fellow out of bed at ten past two. I'll be going to sleep at my desk at school tomorrow."

"If you don't get out of that bed you won't be able to *sit* at your desk tomorrow!"

Perry moaned and pushed himself over the side and shivered out loud so everyone could hear. "It's cold, Dad."

"Put warm clothes on."

"I don't know where they are. I can't see."

"The clothes you wore yesterday, you mutton-head. They'll be on the floor, your mother says, where you dropped them."

"Can I leave my pajamas on? Can I put my clothes over the top?"

"No, you can't. We have no idea how long we shall be, and I'm not having you running round in broad daylight in your pajamas."

"Can I wear m' long pants?"

"Oh, for pity's sake, boy. There *couldn't* be another like you. Wear what you like!"

"Be good, Perry," Mum called. "Your father has a lot on his mind."

"I thought it was the ladies who had to get the babies!"

"And so it is, dear."

"Well, what's he in a fizz for?"

"One of these days, Perry, you might be in the same position and then you'll understand. In the meantime will you please dress without further disturbance? I have stood about enough of it myself."

"It's silly," Perry grumbled. "Did I get born in the middle of the night?"

"No, you didn't. You were born at five in the afternoon."

"Well, why can't this baby get born then, too?"

No answer, not from anyone, just grunts and scufflings on the other side of the wall as if Dad were hopping round on one foot trying to pull a boot on, a very *irritable* sound that sent Perry scuttling for his clothes. Dad had a heavy hand that he didn't use often, but when he did use it, it stung!

"I'm getting dressed, Dad," he wailed. "I am. I am. I'll be ready in no time, you'll see."

Perry flying round the room throwing things off and dragging things on, leaving half the buttons until later, plunging into the wardrobe for his overcoat, old shoes and games in boxes and tobacco tins full of treasures tumbling out on the floor with a clatter, Mum suddenly in the doorway all rugged up with a comb in her hand.

"Hair, Perry."

"Aw, Mum. It'll do."

"*Comb* it, Perry."

Dad was waiting in the passage with a suitcase. "Blow out your candle," he said. "Leave the stuff on the floor, leave it there, leave it there. We'll have to clean it up later. Really, Perry, we shouldn't have to be worrying about you. It's not much to ask of you. To get dressed. To comb your hair. To do it quietly. To be ready."

"All right, dear," Mum said. "You know what you're like yourself when you're pulled out in the middle of the night."

Dad mumbled something or other and Perry blew the candle out and Dad extinguished the light in the passage and struck another match and everybody in line astern started shuffling toward the back of the house. "Watch the mat," Dad said. "Watch the cat dish. Watch the step. Blessed rain. What the tarnation has it got to rain for? As if a man hasn't enough to worry about."

Dad had the door open and it was blustering outside and everything was as black as black.

"Amazing," Dad said. "Hasn't rained since goodness knows when and now down it comes."

"You wanted the rain, Dad."

"I don't want it tonight! You'll have to wait here. I'll have to switch the car lights on or you'll never see your way. Blessed rain. I ask you."

Dad grumbled off into the darkness as if stepping off the edge of the world, maybe never to be heard of again (Man Lost. Falls off Edge of World) and Perry started shivering under Mum's hand, that hand clutching at his shoulder, Mum bearing on him so heavily that he seemed all at once to be supporting half her weight. Perry winced and rammed an elbow into the frame of the door to hold himself there. "Gee, Mum. . . ."

"Sorry, dear."

"Mum, are you all right?"

"Perfectly, dear."

"You're *heavy*."

"Yes, I forgot. Perhaps I thought you were a tree. You're a strong boy. As strong as a tree. . . ." But Mum's weight wasn't going away as suddenly as it had come. "It's nice knowing you're there, my big son. You'll help Dad while I'm away, won't you? Dry the dishes and things. Make your bed. Can you hear the car? Is the engine running?"

"No, Mum."

"He should have it running by now. I hope there's no trouble with the car. There shouldn't be. He serviced it the other day. . . . *Denis!*" Mum called into the night, into the sound of the wind and the rain. "Denis, are you having trouble with the car?"

There was no answer from Dad.

(Man still falling off edge of world. Tumbling.)

"Denis!"

Mum's voice had turned shrill, almost as if she were afraid, which simply could not have been.

Mum afraid?

Mum was brave.

Not that she went out fighting snakes, for instance, or flying airplanes, or driving racing cars, but all the family said she was brave to give up so much to live in a lonely place because Dad believed in simple things. Dad was brave, too. When the man came from the Agricultural Department to look at the farm he said to Dad, "You've got the heart of a lion."

"Dad can't hear you, Mum. It's the wind. It's the rain."

"He hasn't switched the lights on. Why not? *Denis!*"

"I don't think he can hear you, Mum." But Perry knew that Dad should have called her by now even if the car wouldn't run.

"Perry," Mum said, "I want you to see what's wrong." Her weight eased away. "Just now I want to wait quietly here. Step carefully. It'll be slippery on the path."

Mum's weight had gone but a greater weight was

lying upon him in the tone of her voice and the insistent pressure of her hand, a *responsibility* that suddenly he didn't want to carry on his own out into the dark, out into the rain.

"Please, dear," Mum said. "There can't be any danger, you know that. Nothing's there in the night that isn't there in the day. You're a big boy now."

Mum was pushing him in the back. Pushing him out into the night.

"You're a big boy now."

2
A Man Now

Perry was out in the blackness and the rain and the noise of the storm *on his own*. How could it be? Out there with wind tossing through vague masses that were hydrangeas and ferns, on that narrow brick path it was impossible to see and that he could feel only through the soles of his feet and follow only from instinct. A thousand times he had walked up and down it, at least a thousand times, yet had never noticed whether it turned to the left or to the right.

He was out in it and Mum had pushed him there. Mum leaning up against the door.

"Where are you, Dad?"

Perry groping with his hands out in front, rain spilling down his neck, ferns brushing his face like flights of wet birds, wanting to run for the shed at the foot of the path where the car was kept, wanting to get there out of the rain but being alerted to a memory of something in the way. His billy-cart left on the path. Left exactly where?

It was awful not being able to see.

"Dad?"

A wind-blown call came from the house. Mum's call. "Can't you find him? Doesn't he answer?"

"No, Mum."

"Where have you looked?"

"I'm on the path, Mum."

"*Still* on it?"

"I can't see, Mum. It's no good being cross with me."

"Will you go on down to the shed and get out of the rain? I'll bring the hurricane lamp." Mum's shout sounded sharp, almost angry.

"Dad," Perry yelled. "Answer me." Then went blundering on down the path, hoping not to strike his billy-cart, hoping Dad had put it away. "Why don't you answer, Dad? Where are you?"

Dad wasn't in the shed, that shed open to the weather on two sides. The little Morris car with the canvas hood was empty. Perry thumped on it but Dad didn't answer. Even the doors were shut. Dad wasn't at the wheel.

"Dad, where have you gone?"

Was this what night was like? The unexplored world of blackness before dawn. Dad stepping out from the porch and becoming nothing at all. Was there really an edge to the world? Were they stumbling round in the dark at the brink of it?

"Perry!" Mum's faint call shrilled from the house. "Is your father there?"

He felt a sudden, intense longing to be back in bed, to be sound asleep, to be where a fellow at least knew that dreams were only dreams however alarming they might have been for a short time.

"I'm coming, Perry."

Thank goodness for that!

The lamp was on the path, coming down, held high and swinging in Mum's hand. Mum shuffling along carefully, yellow light spilling over her, rain like needles spiking through the glow, sparkling fern fronds in the wind, Perry's heart suddenly thudding as the lamp dipped to the ground as if released from Mum's hand, almost seeming to fall, but it was only Mum bending at the knees as if preparing to lift a weight or utter a prayer. Mum kneeling there in wet light and blackness. Everything looking strange. As if this were a moment separate from the rest of living.

"Perry, come here."

Mum sounded so calm.

Perry didn't want to go, wanted to turn and hide, didn't want the blame.

"Perry. Are you coming?"

He had to go, and there it was as he had guessed it would be, the billy-cart in a tangle at Dad's feet, Dad lying off the path hard against the rocks at the edge of the garden bed, Dad lying only inches from where Perry had groped by, Dad face down, not moving. Oh gee, looking so *different*. A minute ago stepping into the rain, grumbling. Now not moving.

Mum knelt in an unnatural way with her back quite straight, with the lamp at her side, trying to raise Dad by one arm. "Help me, Perry. And get that billy-cart out of the way. Oh, Perry, he told you last night at the dinner table *not* to leave it there. Don't you ever do anything you're told?"

Mum's voice was still so calm, so terribly calm, and Perry couldn't move. Dad's face was in the light now, looking strange; his head cradled in Mum's arm, his eyes closed, blood mixing with rain and trickling from the roots of his hair.

"He's so clumsy in the dark," Mum said, "poor dear. It had to happen some day. Rushing every-where. *Perry, will you throw that beastly billy-cart away!*"

Her change of tone shocked him to move, made

him cry, and he did exactly as she ordered him to do, snatched up the billy-cart with more strength than he dreamed he had and threw it into the hydrangeas, smashing it out into the darkness beyond the light, smashing down branches, crying all the time, "I'm sorry, Mum, I'm sorry, I meant to put it away. I thought Dad had put it away. Mum, is he hurt bad?"

"Am I a doctor? Am I used to this sort of thing? Concussion I suppose. I don't know. Oh, Perry, that it should happen now when there's so little time."

"Mum, I'm sorry, I'm sorry, I'm sorry."

"My suitcase is there. Do you see! My suitcase getting wet. Get it under cover quickly or everything for the baby will be ruined."

"I'm sorry, I'm sorry."

"Of course you are. Run the suitcase down to the car. And don't fall whatever you do. We're relying on you now. And don't cry any more. It's done, it's done; it's no good crying now." Her voice was following him as he stumbled to the shed hugging the suitcase in his arms, her voice getting louder, shouting, and following him all the way. "Put it on the front seat. That's the boy. Switch on the parking lights while you're there. You know the switch; you've done it before. It'll help us to see. Then back again quickly, Perry. Back again quickly, please.

You've got to be a man now. My big son. Strong like
a tree. Can't you find those parking lights? Good
heavens, Perry, at the bottom of the dashboard; you
know where. The little knob second from the left.
Perry, are you all right?"

"Yes, Mum."

But he was cold and his nose was running and he
was wet and he was knocking his elbows on things
and banging his knees and couldn't think properly
because her voice was drumming on in his head and
it wasn't the second knob from the left but the second from the right and if Dad was sick with concussion who was going to drive the car? Mum hadn't
driven for ages. Mum didn't have a license any
more. She was a *terrible* driver, like the ladies in the
jokes that comedians made. They'd be going nowhere in the car. They'd be staying right at home.
That stupid baby would have to wait. If it had done
without a mother until now it could do without a
mother until tomorrow.

"That's fine, Perry."

What was fine? What was she talking about? What
was she yelling about?

"That little bit of light makes all the difference,
Perry. Now hurry back, please. Your father's getting
wet. So am I."

Back where? He didn't want to go anywhere, except back to bed, but found himself in the rain with water in his hair and in his eyes, water running down his neck and back from the cuffs of his sleeves, and Dad still lying with his head in Mum's arm, her other hand stroking his brow.

Mum seemed to be bending from the middle with a look of awful strain.

"Help me lift him, Perry. We'll have to drag him to the shed. We can do it, I know we can. That's the boy; take his other arm. Now pull him onto the path. Pull harder, Perry."

It wasn't like being awake. Not at all. It was not like anything he had known before. Who would have guessed that a world like this was lying outside the back door?

"I'm pulling, Mum."

Panting beside her, heaving and straining together, jerking Dad onto the path inches at a time.

"I'm sorry, Mum. I'm so sorry."

"It's done, Perry. No good regretting now." But Mum moved suddenly away and stood above him with her eyes closed and hands clenched each into the other. "I can't," she said.

Perry with rain beating on him, looking up. "Can't what, Mum?"

Mum was like someone different, like a stranger. Even her voice was different, saying many things that didn't form into words.

"You'll have to do it for me, Perry."

How could it have been real?

"All your life, Perry, I have done things gladly for you. Now you must do something for me. You're a big boy, my strong son."

"Mum, I can't lift Dad. . . ."

"You must try. It's too much for me."

"Of course it's not, Mum."

"Mothers have to be careful when their babies are about to be born. I have said to you, we're relying on you; you must be the man."

Mum was walking slowly away, slowly down the path toward the glow of taillights in the shed; leaves and twigs and rain and Mum against a red glow leaving Perry on his own with Dad.

It was *ridiculous*.

"*Mum!*"

She leaned against the car as if intending to wait for him there.

"Bend to it, Perry."

Dad looked so limp, so heavy. Dad looked far too big to be moved by half a dozen Perrys. Taking a step from the porch into the two o'clock world was like leaving yourself behind, was like waking up somewhere and finding that you weren't there.

Dad lying flat on his back on the path with rain spitting on the hot glass of the hurricane lamp only inches from his feet, that smoky yellow flame flickering and flaring like a candle in a drafty room. Dad looking awful, looking so helpless lying there.

But Dad was the man who swung an ax and steered the plow and leaped bareback onto the draft horse and went flopping, galloping, bouncing all over the hillside laughing with excitement like a boy, waving his hat in the air like a stockman, acting the fool. He was a terrific Dad.

Was that the Dad who had his hit head on a stone?

Suddenly Perry was pulling like mad, dragging at Dad in spasms, each spasm another inch or two, repeatedly slipping and thudding on his backside but instantly pulling again. Getting covered in mud, getting drenched, sweat pouring out of him, getting hotter and hotter but becoming stronger and stronger the hotter he got. Pulling on Dad, dragging him, shouting to Mum, "I'm coming, Mum. See? See? I'm doing it, Mum."

The lamp that had been near Dad's feet began looking far away; rain was still sputtering on it but it was too far off to hear. Rain was drumming on the iron roof of the shed and Dad's face was turning red in the taillight glow. Perry was groaning into the tanbark on the shed floor and Mum's hand was resting on his head.

"Good boy."

It was done. Gee willikins, it was done. A wheel of the car was bearing against his shoulder and his hair was like wet rag in his eyes and his throat was sore from gulping at cold air.

"Good boy. My strong son."

He had done it. Dragged a big man all that way. On his own. Yet somehow it was like a dream.

Mum had opened a door of the car.

"Now to get him in. On the back seat with him, Perry. Up you get. Don't allow yourself to go cold."

He looked up at her, not believing her.

"Come on, Perry. He can't be left here. Prop him against the door, then get inside and I'll help you pull him through."

"Mum, I can't. . . ."

"Of course you can. The hardest job's done. This is easy. Hook your elbows under his armpits."

Maybe not like a dream. Maybe like a storybook with characters he couldn't believe in. But he was doing as she ordered. Somehow he was struggling with Dad into position against the opening of the door and clambering over him into the back seat. All he wanted to do was sink into the seat and lie in a huddle of aches and pains. But Mum was prodding him.

"Mum. . . . There's not enough room. . . ."

"Plenty of room. Open the door behind you. The hard work's done. This is easy."

"But you're not helping me, Mum. You're only making out you are."

Something about her manner made him heave again until he thought that his insides would break and all the time she was driving him on as someone without heart might urge a small horse to draw a huge load.

"Good boy."

What did that mean?

He was down on his knees in the tanbark with Mum's hands on his shoulders for a few moments of intense and painful pressure. But Mum was saying something through her hands; hurting him and loving him through her hands; saying *thank you* in one of those strange grown-up ways.

"Good boy."

Then he was drooping on his own, almost falling on his face, no hands to love him or hurt him, no hands to hold him up, and doors of the car started slamming and Mum said, "Get in the back with Dad. You can make room but see he doesn't fall. Did

you notice the car key, Perry? I think Dad had it in
his hand. Did you see it anywhere?"

"No. . . ."

"I'll get the spare."

So he had to get in the car. So he had to crawl up
over the step and grope in beside Dad, Dad propped
up like a huge limp doll. Had Perry propped him
there? There was nothing to remember except aches
and nothing now except a dreamlike daze, all wet
and muddy and clammy with sweat, and a giddiness
that might have meant he had dragged the strength
of a man out of the body of a boy.

3
The World Outside

Mum's face appeared outside with the hurricane lamp held close, the glass raised, puffing out the flame with full cheeks flecked with rain. Over her shoulder were towels.

"Is your father waking?"

"No, Mum."

She sat in the driver's seat, that bucket seat, sat stiffly there as if she had no intention of making a further move, and Perry struggled with the framework of a question he was almost afraid to ask.

"Take a towel, Perry. Dry yourself, and dry your father if you can."

"Mum, you couldn't be going to drive?"

He heard her draw a deep breath. Over the sound

of rain he heard it. And her shoulders moved with the breath, moved up and sank down. Then she reached for the light switch and everything became blackness.

"Are you using the towel, Perry?"

For a time everything remained dark and cramped and strange as if Mum was still making up her mind. What was going on in the blackness?

"Perry. You understand that I've got to take the car."

He didn't understand; but was afraid to say it.

"You heard me, Perry."

"Yes, Mum."

"We'll be all right. God will take care of us. He will not allow us to come to any harm."

The engine started grinding over and over and over with tired groans until it fired with a roar.

"Mum," Perry shouted. "Have we got to go?"

She appeared not to hear because the headlights suddenly and starkly illuminated the timber wall, the tools leaning there and the shelves bearing Dad's orderly jars of nuts and bolts and nails, the light flooding all around, edged with glowing clouds of exhaust smoke and puddles and sparkling rain.

"What's the hurry, Mum? Can't we wait until Dad feels better?"

"Be quiet, Perry."

"Mum, you always bang into things. You always break things."

The engine sighed back to an idle and Mum started fiddling with the gears and steering wheel and handbrake as if she were pretending to drive, started shifting in her seat restlessly as if not certain whether to make herself comfortable or put her head out the side, worrying about backing perhaps, whether she should go all the way to the gate in reverse or turn the car on the curve like Dad.

"Mum, I'm frightened. . . ."

"Don't be absurd, Perry."

The car bounded toward the wall in front almost as if it had leaped of its own accord and Mum savagely stopped it, obviously startled and unnerved, then went back to her fiddling with the gears and Perry shut his eyes and clenched his hands and pushed up closer to Dad.

Not much sense pressing up to Dad. "Gee, Dad, what'd you go and fall for? Mum's in such a tearing hurry all the time. She always reckons you're the one in the hurry, or me, but it's her. Why can't she wait awhile? The baby'll still be at the hospital in the morning, won't it?"

But Dad didn't move except to the jerking of the car, a jerking that broke Perry's eyes open in alarm, and Mum was going backward this time, the engine making too much noise. Dad must have been dead to the world or he'd have been leaping up and down and screaming about what she was doing to his car. But Mum didn't seem to be thinking of Dad. She should have been looking after him, fanning him or something, giving him brandy or something. She didn't seem to be thinking of him at all.

Mum had the car out in the open going backward, weaving and bumping all over the place, headlights sweeping frighteningly over house and garden and paddock as they never did when Dad was reversing the car. It was like something that might have happened in a fairground that no one genuinely had to worry about, because it couldn't possibly be real.

Rain was blustering on the hood, the windshield wipers were flicking in a frantic way, and Mum was talking to herself with her head stuck out the side and had missed the curve on the drive and was backing downhill into the gully instead of heading the proper way. The gate was uphill, not down. Perry in an instant thought of that gully, the long slope getting steeper and steeper, thought of Mum careering down into it, faster and faster backward, crashing backward into a tree.

But the car wasn't moving except by the tail, slewing its tail from side to side, wagging it, wheels spinning. Mum was trying to go forward, but wasn't going anywhere, not even backward any more.

"Mum, what are you doing?"

She snatched for the handbrake and the engine note faded and Mum seemed to sink into depths of the little bucket seat that Perry had never noticed before. Mum seemed to sink almost out of sight. Or else she shrank.

"Perry, you're not helping me. I asked you particularly to be quiet."

"Mum, you're off the drive."

"I know."

"Mum, you're in the grass."

"Yes, Perry."

"You should have waited for Dad."

"Perry, will you please be quiet or I think I'll scream."

Mum simply went on sitting there, or shrinking there, and the horrible night made its horrible noises and everything was silly, everything was stupid.

"Perry."

He answered her sullenly, shivering from nerves and from cold. "Yes. . . ."

"Do you think you could push? Do you think you could get out and push?"

Something inside him made a sniggering sound.

"The car, Mum?"

"Yes, dear; the car. It won't need much. Just a helping hand."

He thought about it, distantly, as he might think of topping the class or breaking the four-minute mile. "Push the car?"

"Yes, dear."

"Push it where? Can't we wait for Dad?"

"Your father may be unconscious for hours."

"No, he won't be."

She sighed. "He may be quite ill."

"No, he isn't."

"He needs medical attention. I'm very worried about your father."

"I didn't think you were. It's the rotten baby all the time."

That was *telling* her.

In a moment Mum shifted her hands to the top of the steering wheel and used its leverage to lift herself straight again.

"Perry. . . ."

But he felt cold and hard and indifferent to her. It was something new; a strange feeling. Then she leaned on the steering wheel, leaned there a while, her head pillowed on her hands, a stranger to him, seen against the glow of headlights on rain.

"Perry, this is difficult. You don't seem to realize. You seem to have gone away from me somehow. I thought I had made the urgency clear; not only for the baby but for your father, too. The baby will not wait."

"Someone else can have it then."

"No, darling. No one else can."

"Who's to stop them? I won't."

"Perry, we must have our own baby. You know these things. It's not that you haven't been told."

"Haven't been told what?"

"Perry, you couldn't have forgotten."

"Forgotten what?"

She made a strange sound through her nose. "You didn't take it in, did you? You didn't understand."

"Sure I did. You asked me to push the car. But I can't push the car."

"No, Perry, no; not the car, you can be so *deaf*, so *busy* all the time; the only things you hear are what you want to hear. A mother prepares for her baby for a long while. For her particular baby. We've told you."

"Yeh, Mum, I know."

"Are you *sure* you know?"

"Yeh, yeh."

"Then you can understand that the baby is with us already. In this car. Now."

The engine was idling. The windshield wipers clicked back and forth. The lights beamed through rain across the garden. No one was with him in the car but Mum and Dad. Poor old Dad in a heap. And Mum stiff and straight and upright again.

"You haven't thought it through, have you?" she said. "You haven't got round really to *grasping* it."

His throat felt dry. "I don't know what you mean, Mum."

"You haven't noticed any difference about me, have you?"

"I don't know what you mean, Mum." He was shivering and frightened. "Don't talk like this, Mum. There's no baby here. Really there's not, Mum. Don't talk like this. I'll push the car." He fumbled the door open and plunged into the rain and slithered to the back of the car. "I'm pushing, Mum," he yelled.

The sound of her voice was almost a cry. "Oh, Perry. . . ." But the engine revved and the wheels spun and mud sprayed out past him from the tires in showers. The car would never move, never move, until someone brought a tractor or Dad hitched up the horse and pulled it to firm ground. How could Perry push any more? All he wanted to do was cry.

Mum had come and possessed him by the shoulders and enclosed him securely within her arms, within the folds of her heavy coat, and she stood with him in the rain, ignoring the rain. Stood with

him beside the car, soft earth inches deep, soft spring
grass inches high. How strange was the world outside
when a fellow should have been in bed.

"Mum, you've got the car way off the drive."

"I know, dear."

"I can't push any more."

"No, dear. I don't expect you to."

"Mum, I tried. I'm sorry about the billy-cart. I'm
sorry about Dad."

"I know, I know."

"It's all my fault. I'm always doing things the
wrong way. I can't help it if I don't understand."

Still she held to him but found his hands and
pressed them to her side, a strange thing for her to
do in the way that she did it; stranger still was the
silence that she eventually broke. "That's where the
baby is. Under your hands."

He started thinking about it. Listening to her
voice and thinking at the same time. Remembering
things. Of course he had known; yet somehow
hadn't known. He had been told; of course he had
been told; yet somehow the pressure against his
hands was a surprise, a huge, round surprise.

"That's where our baby has grown. Day by day.
Growing with us. That's why our baby is ours.
That's why you belong, too. You were there once.
We all belong to each other; Dad and you and me

and our baby in there waiting to be born. Our baby is ready, just as you were ready once."

A strange feeling; strange words; they really were.

"You let everyone know you wanted to be born. And you were. You were much more impatient than this little one here. This little girl or this little boy. That's why mothers and fathers love their children so. The first one very specially—even if he doesn't understand. And all the others, just the same."

Still the rain. Still the little car in the mud. Mum still with her coat around him.

"Our new baby under your hands is *anxious* to be born."

"And that's what the hurry is?"

"That's it, dear."

He was shivering against her, trembling against her, overawed.

"The baby's in there? Inside? Been there all the time? Every day?"

"Since January."

"Mum, it's October now."

"Yes, October now."

"All the year? Every day. Our baby in there. Belonging to us already. Why didn't you say?"

"I thought you knew, and it seemed so obvious to me. I suppose it always seems obvious to mothers. I can't begin to imagine why you didn't see. Oh, to be a boy."

"Mum, isn't it strange?"

"No, darling. Where else could a baby be? Wonderful, but not strange. And that's why our baby can't be born without me. It's why we hurry when the time comes around."

Perry stood wrapped in Mum's arms, with the baby under his hands. She mightn't have thought it was strange, but it was. Life was there, under his hands, his brother or his sister, invisible, out of reach. Unimaginable.

"Hullo, baby," Perry called, "hullo you in there. You should've picked a better night for it. You should've, you know. Don't you get the weather report in there?"

4
Traps Set.
Baits Laid

Mum perched herself on the back seat beside Dad and mopped herself with a towel. Perry mopped himself too, then sat up to the wheel making sure his hands were hidden from her because then he could pretend to drive. A forbidden pleasure. Never was he allowed to sit at the wheel with the engine alive, the engine throbbing. "No," someone would always say, "it's too dangerous, Perry." Had Mum forgotten the rule? Outside yellow rain crossed the light beams and glistened on grass and Mum seemed to be laughing to herself through her nose with a noise that sounded like Dad's name. Probably it was not a laugh at all.

As if Perry had never properly known Mum before, or Dad, as if a private and secret door had opened where he had not suspected a door to be. As if the problems of being a grown-up might have been as difficult as the problems of being a boy. Mum's "laugh" was a disturbing sound.

"Perry. Can you reach the accelerator pedal?"

He thought he must have imagined it but Mum repeated herself as if she had realized his surprise. "Can you or can't you?"

"Yes, Mum."

"The lights are going down. I think we have to run the engine faster."

"You mean press the pedal, Mum?"

With a tremble in his foot he made the engine roar and the rain turned silvery in the brightening beam and the white walls of the house showed up through the trees and he had one hand on the wheel and the other on the gear change and it was like doing forty miles an hour.

"Like that, Mum?"

"That's the idea, but a little less noise. And don't touch the gears. Don't put your hands where they shouldn't be."

She had read his mind again though it had been only a *pretend*. Pretending he was driving out, out through the mud, no trouble at all. Pretending they were on their way to the hospital, Perry to the rescue at the wheel.

Mr. Perry Benson Esquire, man, car-driver, rescuer, the fellow who always knew exactly what to do even though he might never have done it before.

"Mum, how are we going to get there in a hurry now?"

"I don't know."

"Mum, what's going to happen if we don't get there?"

"I'm not ready to think about it."

"Would it mean the baby wouldn't be born?"

"It will be born no matter where we are."

He tried to look into the rear vision mirror so that he might see her without turning round, but the angle of the mirror was set too high.

"Mum, how soon have we got to get there?"

"I can't say. Perhaps an hour."

"But it's twelve miles."

"Yes, darling, twelve miles. It might as well be a hundred and twelve. It's too far."

"Wouldn't have taken long in the car though."

"No."

"Well, why did we start out so soon?"

She sighed. "Because there are times when we can't be sure if the baby is coming. The mother has the feeling, that's all. It might happen in an hour, or in a few minutes, or perhaps not until next day. This is one of those times. Perry, you must let me think.

You must stop talking. And ease the engine off a little; you're running it much too hard."

Mum's voice had changed, had turned impatient, and the exciting sense of sharing as an equal in a drama of the adult world went slipping away into the cold. He was Perry again, eleven years old again, down near the bottom of the class again (no one ever *said* it but he *knew*), a nuisance again, to be seen and not heard. The Perry who had left the billy-cart forgotten on the path where Dad could trip and fall. . . .

"Wake up, Dad. Come on, Dad." But reaching Dad when he was unconscious was like trying to shout across a hundred miles. Reaching him by talking or reaching him by thinking, just the same; *nothing* was there. "Gee, Dad, shake a leg. Are you sure you haven't gone to sleep or something? Are you sure you're not dreaming you're in bed? You couldn't have hit yourself *that* hard. We didn't even hear you fall. . . ."

Mum had started talking. "I'm not doing it thoughtlessly, Perry. It's not easy for me. I hate to ask it of you."

"Yes, Mum." Was he already guessing what she was about to say?

"I'd feel much better if someone could get to a telephone."

Yeh; he had guessed it. Yet in a way he had not been able to believe that she'd actually set him to it. "Me, Mum? You want *me* to go to a telephone?"

"Yes, dear."

Did she really know what she was asking? The phone at Mr. Morgan's house, that was half a mile. The phone where Walter Piper lived, that was twice as far. The public phone in the township, that was two whole miles. . . .

Gee, Mum, it's dark out there. Please, Mum, not on my own. In all that rain. In all that dark. All that way to go.

"Did you say something, Perry?"

"I can't go to Mr. Morgan's, Mum. And everywhere else is much too far."

"I know what I'm asking, Perry. It's a taxi we want, and the doctor, and the only way we can get them is through Mr. Morgan's phone."

"Not Mr. Morgan, Mum. I couldn't go there."

"It's the nearest phone, dear, by a long way."

"But it's dark, Mum."

"Take the hurricane lamp and you'll be fine. If you hurry it won't take long, only ten minutes or so. We've got to get help, darling, and we can get it there, only ten minutes away."

"He's a horrible man—"

"Because we don't see eye to eye doesn't make him

horrible. Perhaps he thinks we're horrible, too. But we're not, are we?"

"Dad says he wouldn't ask him for the time of day."

"Fathers can be wrong sometimes. The same as boys." Her hand was touching his shoulder. "Take the matches. I've hung the lamp in the shed. Light it in the corner out of the wind. And carry the matches with you in case you need them again." Her hand was still on his shoulder shaking the matches at his ear. "I must stay with your father. How can I leave him as he is? And it's too far for me. If I slip or fall, as I easily could, I could harm our baby. And that would be terrible. Mothers have to be careful for you even before you're born."

But he didn't want to move.

"You must hurry, my big son, my brave boy. The taxi and Dr. Hearn. Is that clear? Make sure everyone knows exactly what the situation is. A baby coming and your father hurt. We'll leave the car lights on and the engine running until you have your lamp. Off you go."

Mum was breathing against his ear, holding those matches there. Why couldn't they have left him asleep in bed? What would have been so terrible about that? Couldn't they have quietly crept away? Creeping quietly down the path together Dad mightn't have tripped at all. An empty house in the morning would be nothing. Nothing to this.

Suddenly rain was in his face again. Suddenly he was floundering through rain and grass again, match box clenched in his hand. Groping into that rotten shed with his spirits down in his boots but having to reach up for the lamp so dimly seen, having to stretch to his toes, having to jump to get it down.

Mum, it's cruel.

Perry to the rescue; *Mr. Perry Benson Esquire*; it's not pretending now.

Perry to the rescue; having to hoof it; not going by car.

An engine in the billy-cart and Perry could drive.

Imagine sitting in the billy-cart with an engine pop-popping. Imagine sitting there *driving* uphill. Brrrr-rrr-rrr. But the rotten old billy-cart was in the hydrangeas, thrown away. Probably broken now. Kids like Perry never had billy-carts you could sit in and drive. Only billy-carts you had to push or pull or urge down hills. Nothing *ever* that went on its own.

Perry huddling in the corner with the lamp glass raised, striking match after match waiting for one to burn, hoping that every one would fail, hoping that this would be the way, praying for gusts of wind to blow them all out. But the lamp was alight, the rotten thing was burning bright, and he was plodding back into the rain round the curve of the drive, Mum calling, "Bless you, darling. You're a brave boy." Then the car lights blinked out and the engine switched off and it was like waking up again with alarm. Waking up to nothing when it should have been a place he knew. Leaving him with a touch of giddiness as if something solid underneath had been cut away.

Outside his own little yellow pool what was there? How could it be the same as day? In daylight Mr. Morgan's house was half a mile. Out of the gate and up the hill and over the top and down the other side. That was all. Not far. Trees all the way. Gum trees hanging over the road joining from side to side making an arch up there, a long arch. Like a tunnel it was in the day with sunlight breaking through and splashing on the road.

Sunlight splashing on the road changing shape all the time. A magic carpet that never flew.

And birds. And insects in swarms. And rabbits scuttling. All warm and alive. Nothing spoiling it except Mr. Morgan's house if Mr. Morgan was outside. When he wasn't there Perry went skipping on his way to school, nothing spoiling it at all. Or 'used to skip. He was eleven now.

Surly old man reckoning he owned the world.

Surly old man spoiling things for a boy. Gate with a notice on: "Private. Keep Out." Fences with barbed wire on, lots of strands. Peaches in summertime nowhere near the road. Apples in the autumn where boys wouldn't dare to climb. Notices nailed to trees: "Traps set. Baits laid." To foil the foxes who fancied chicken for breakfast. But foxes didn't get caught. Dogs got caught. Trusting dogs like Oliver who wriggled under the fence wagging his tail but never came home. That rotten old man.

If Oliver were alive they'd go together now and Perry wouldn't be alone; yellow pool of light to step in; yellow pool of light moving through the dark out through the gate and onto the road; Perry in the pool all on his own. How could the world outside the light be the same as in the day?

Mum, you wouldn't *really* send me into the dark on my own? With rain coming down? And wind blowing? And noises all around?

Dad should have remembered the billy-cart was there. And, Mum, you should have taken more care. You should have backed out straight. You shouldn't have got off the drive. What a stupid thing to do. I didn't want a baby anyway. Everything was right the way we were. It was nice being just three. And what if it's a girl? Tell me, what are we going to do with a girl? Fancy having a baby and taking pot luck on what it's going to be. If it's a girl I reckon I'll die.

The rain's heavy, Mum. All wet, Mum. My feet are wet, Mum. Always getting wet feet when it rains. Why doesn't Dad send our boots to the bootmaker like other dads do? Mending them himself. He doesn't do them properly, Mum. Why haven't we got things other people have like switches on the wall and lights everywhere? The kids at school reckon Dad's a crank. Making us live like we were in the olden days fifty years ago. Fancy having to go to Mr. Morgan's. Why haven't we got a phone of our own? Fancy making me go to that horrible old man.

Perry in his little pool of yellow, running up the road.

5
Over the Top

Half a mile to Mr. Morgan's. Up the hill and over the top and down the other side. Half a mile when the sun was lighting up the day, but more like miles now. Everything wet and black. Everything roaring with wind. Miles and miles. Little yellow lamp flickering and flaring, blowing out soot. Sooting up the glass. Glass spattering and hissing with rain splashing on it. Great big dollops of rain falling from the trees. Trees like giants as tall as night standing in rows, leg to leg, side by side, bombarding him with dollops of rain as big as stones. Giants sometimes stepping back a stride, or slipping closer, as he floundered by, Perry catching them from the corner of his eye.

Don't you touch me, trees. You stay there. You're not supposed to move around. You're not allowed.

Over the top and down the other side where shapeless creatures that should have lived in dreams were out hunting for boys who should have been in bed. Creatures with too many heads and too many feet and horrible wailing cries. Two A.M. *creatures*.

I'm hurrying, Mum, like you said.

Not because I'm scared.

Lamp jigging up and down. Don't you go out, lamp. If you go out I think I'll die.

Golly, Mr. Morgan, you'd better be at home. What'll I do if you've gone away? I'll kill you, Mr. Morgan, if you're not there. I'll let out all your chickens and call all the foxes, *coo-eee you foxes*, all the lady foxes with lots of kids at home wanting chicken for breakfast. Mr. Morgan, don't you dare not be at home because Perry's coming to bang at your door. Perry from way back there.

Perry who cried at your gate when Oliver didn't come home and you said go away Benson Boy, be a man. If I had been *half* as big as you I wouldn't have gone. No. I'd have thrashed you until you couldn't stand. Hurting a little dog when he never did anyone harm. Only loving everyone. Only licking people on the hand. And now I can't have another. It's not worth the heartbreak, Dad says. Pets always getting killed somehow. Why do they ever get born if they've always gotta die?

What do you want to chain your gate for? Great big chain you've got there. Great big hook. Great big gate. You've locked me out, Mr. Morgan. We don't chain our gate. Our gate's open wide for friends to come inside. Great big chain. Who you frightened of? Of little dogs and kids coming in the dark?

"Mr. Morgan!"

Can't you hear me calling you? I can't shift your rotten old chain. You've gone and pulled it too tight. It's Perry at your gate out here in the rain getting blown around, out here yelling for you.

"Mr. Morgan!"

You're awful not answering me, not hearing, making me climb your gate because who can climb your fence with barbed wire strung everywhere? Climbing your great high gate. You wouldn't put barbed wire on top of it, Mr. Morgan? You wouldn't do *that*. Because if I get hooked or drop my lamp, because if I get caught on barbed wire I think I'll die.

Gee willikens lucky for you Mr. Morgan you've put no wire up here if you had I'd killed you true.

But what you want to build your house for way down there in the dark, way down there in the trees,

way down there away from the road so you can't
hear anybody outside? What do you want to do that
for making me go all this way plowing through all
your mud and wet high grass?

You wake up and you stir your bones. Don't you
go pulling the blankets over your head you horrible
old man. It's Perry banging out here on the side of
your house, banging on your windows and at your
door, it's Perry Benson you've got out here.

"Mr. Morgan!"

Please wake up. Please be at home for me.

"Mr. Morgan!"

What about my Mum? What about my Dad?
What are you going to do about me out here all on
my own?

Have I got to go on farther now? To Walter
Piper's house? Another half mile? And they're home
from school with the mumps at Walter's house. You
rotten old man making me go on another half mile,
all that way off the main road, all that way through
the bush to Walter Piper's house and when I get
there they'll be waiting at the gate for me, waiting
there to jump on me, those rotten old mumps, and
Dad said don't you bring them home to this house.
You give me the mumps, young fellow, and I'll tan
your hide and hang it from a tree. But I can't walk

on into town. All that way. One and a half miles more in the dark with m' lamp sooting up and all, and the wind and the rain and the noises everywhere, all on me own.

By gee, Mr. Morgan, can't you hear me banging on your door?

I ran, Mum, ran and ran all the way, but you didn't tell me what to do if he wasn't at home.

Oh, Mum, he won't answer the door, that rotten old man.

6
Big Fat Bully Man

"Someone chasing you, boy? Ay? Got devils after you, boy?"

Mr. Morgan was away up there with a bright brim of light spilling from his hand onto the ground, spilling onto Perry like a barrel of light emptying over him, pouring all around, lighting up a rifle, a long rifle poking from his side, lighting it up until it was the largest rifle anyone had ever seen. If it had not been Mr. Morgan, Perry would have leaped up into his arms. But leaping up there and getting hugged safe by *him* would be the end of the world.

"No one's chasing you, Benson Boy. There's no one out there."

Turn that rifle away, Mr. Morgan; maybe I would leap up into your arms if it wasn't there; I don't like

that rifle drillin' at me, all ready to go bang here and bang there, me gettin' in the way of it all the time. Gettin' shot full of holes. Arrgh. Big holes and little holes. Arrrrgh. Whatchoo want a rifle for?

"Well, Benson Boy, I'm still waiting to hear why you're banging at my door at this ungodly hour. What are you doing here yelling and jumping up and down? Ay? Been making so much noise you haven't the breath left to make any more?"

"Arrgh."

"That noise conveys nothing to me, boy. Or is it that you want to come inside? Please do. Standing here we'll catch our deaths of cold if you haven't already caught yours. Talk about drowned child. You're *wet*, Benson Boy."

The rifle barrel turned into the shape of a hand and drew him through the door. A light switch clicked and Perry was in an almost empty room he had never seen before.

"Stand there. On the mat. Don't move. You'll flood me out of house and home. What have you been doing? Swimming all the way?"

Mr. Morgan hung his flashlight to a hook on the wall and propped his rifle against a wooden chair and wore white pajamas with red stripes and a huge smooth stomach with gray hairs on it bursting through. Almost going pop. Perry's eyes almost going pop, too.

"Well? Well? What are you doing here? Are you going to tell me or am I supposed to guess?"

"Arrgh. Arrgh."

"That's interesting, Benson Boy, but isn't there anything you'd care to add? Like good morning or good night? Perhaps you have tickets to sell? Raffle for the fete at school? Nothing less important, I'm sure, would bring you to my door at five past three."

"The car, Mr. Morgan. We've got it stuck in the mud."

"You have? Well, that could be an interesting beginning. Where is it stuck?"

"At home, Mr. Morgan."

"And you've come all this distance in all this dark in all this thundering rain to tell me that?"

"But it is, Mr. Morgan. It's stuck. And Mum's in it and Dad's in it and they're stuck and the baby's in it, too, and you guess *where*? And Dad fell over my billy-cart and knocked his head and Mum's got to get to hospital maybe in a minute or maybe in a day and she tried to drive the car and got stuck and the baby's in an awful tearin' hurry Mum said and what are we going to do because Dad fell over my billy-cart and knocked his head and Mum said run to Mr.

Morgan's and ask him to use the phone and I ran and ran and couldn't open your rotten gate and I thought I'd get caught on your rotten barbed wire and you wouldn't come to your rotten door and I got scared because I didn't want to walk all the way into town because they got the mumps at Walter Piper's and Mum says someone's got to ring Doctor Hearn and the taxi because we're stuck and Dad fell over my billy-cart. . . ."

Perry standing in a pool of water, Perry panting, waving his arms around, his lamp at his feet pouring out smoke.

"And that," said Mr. Morgan from away up there, "is putting it in a nutshell, as it were."

"We're *stuck*, Mr. Morgan."

"I gathered that, boy."

"You're the nearest telephone."

"I am? Well, it's not a distinction I'll be advertising, no sir."

"Are you teasing me? I don't want no teasing. I want you using your telephone, please."

"You do? All right then, we'll let the doctor know. But you'll stay where you are, you'll stand there and not move. And blow out that filthy lamp before it chokes us all."

"The taxi, Mr. Morgan, the taxi, the taxi, you didn't say the taxi."

"A taxi here? At this godforsaken hour? Blow out that lamp, boy. Filthy thing. Soot everywhere."

So Perry blew out his lamp and when he looked up that horrible man had gone as if he had never been there. "Mr. Morgan, the taxi, the taxi, what are we going to do about the taxi?"

But the room remained bare and the walls did not reply.

"Mr. Morgan, *please.*"

That horrible man. That horrible huge hairy old man telling him to stand, telling him not to move, leaving him in a puddle growing bigger all the time. Water dribbling down his back and trickling down his middle. *Cold.* Rain outside still pattering on the ground. Wind still blustering through the open door. Standing all alone in a room so bare when he should have been at home asleep in bed. White plaster walls. Rifle leaning against a chair. What did he want a rifle for? Frightening the living daylights out of a boy. Egg crates stacked upon the floor. Broken eggs and yellow smears. Ink-stained table over there, fluttering papers held down with an apple core. Huge, huge apple core. A horrible room for a horrible man. No curtains at the window panes. Cold black window panes. Bare light globe hanging from a cord. Mean old man. Not calling Perry by his name. It's Perry you've got here who's walked past your rotten old house for five whole years and never been inside before.

"All right, Benson Boy. The doctor knows."

Mr. Morgan clopping to the door in rubber boots and black rainwear.

"The taxi, Mr. Morgan. Gee. . . ."

"No use chasing rainbows, boy. Only wasting time. Out you go."

Perry was picked up and put down. Out in the rain again, his lamp in his hand, lamp without light, lamp all black, rain streaming down, wind blowing wild, Mr. Morgan blocking the door.

"*Mr. Morgan, go where, go where?*" Perry thumped him with his fist, banged him with his hand, kicked him with a hard toe, and bawled, "My Mum said I had to get a taxi."

The door slammed and the big fat man was on the outside with a big fat hand on Perry's shoulder pushing him along, flashlight beam sparkling through the rain. Puddles and plants and weeds and blackness all around. "Young fellow, you have a shocking opinion of me. I don't feel flattered, not at all. Am I the sort of man who would send a boy with worries like yours into the night on his own?"

"Yes," Perry yelled. "Yes, you are."

"Bless me. Horns and all? And what do you think I'm doing now?"

"I don't know what you're doing," Perry bawled, "and stop pushing me, you big fat bully man."

"You've got spirit. I'm surprised." They had come to a door, a huge and padlocked door with puddles everywhere, and Mr. Morgan's hand bore more heavily down. "Stand there, or I'll leave you to it, yes, by George. You've got spirit, but you are intolerably rude. Like your father. Hold the torch while I unlock the door."

"Why?"

"Do as you're told."

The flashlight came thrusting into Perry's other hand. Mr. Morgan so tall, so stern, so huge. Like a steamroller. Like a storm. Mr. Morgan fiddling with keys. "Hold the light steady. Hold it, boy." Mr. Morgan hauling on the door, shoulder to it, squealing it on rusty rails, sliding it away into the wall. Inside a rotary hoe, a tractor, and the motor car. Perry did not want to believe. Horrible men were never kind.

"All right, Benson Boy, don't stand in the rain. Get under cover. Get in the car. And don't ask why, because I'm sure you know."

Perry sighed an imitation of the sighs he heard from Dad when plants came up that were not the seeds he had thought were in the ground. Sighed, and climbed into the car like climbing steps to reach a high stool, an ornate saloon built long before he was born. Perhaps built before Dad was born. Perhaps built before everybody was born. Perhaps so old it had always *been.*

"Give me some light, boy. Shine it over here so I can see."

Mr. Morgan over there, in the back, clearing out the seat. Tossing heaps of old hessian bags and old egg trays and old tools to the darkness outside, rubbing over the seat with a rag, knocking spider webs down, grunting, "It'll do." Then reaching over a hand to push at levers on the steering wheel, to flick switches and pull knobs and waggle at gears. All very strange.

"Don't you touch anything, boy. It'll bite."

I'm eleven, Mr. Morgan; not a little boy. I've sat at the wheel of a car before. I've even pressed the pedals. I don't have to be told.

Mr. Morgan up the front somewhere, almost in the rain, cranking at a handle, violently lurching the car as if trying to throw it bodily off the ground. Perry with awful thoughts of the handle held firmly in Mr. Morgan's mighty hand and the car spinning round it madly in the air. The engine roaring now, everything frantically shaking up and down.

Mr. Morgan arriving in bulk like an express train, enormously, squashing the seat down, squashing

down the whole car, commanding it to behave itself simply by his being there. Which it did, quietly and smoothly, humming, until Mr. Morgan drove it grandly out into the night as if driving a carriage with horses prancing at the end of reins.

Gee, Mum, it's the car, that's what it is, the extra super special car Dad says the Governor used to drive forty years ago. The one Mr. Morgan bought at auction in 1951 for the price of a pushbike; isn't that what Dad says? Because no one else was brave enough to bid against him because they took him for a big bad-tempered millionaire. The car the Governor went to Parliament in, Mum, and drove to the Melbourne Cup back in the olden days, in his plumes an' all, with his chauffeur an' all, with his Lady sitting up beside him in ostrich feathers. That's what I'm sitting in, Mum. Wow.

Sitting up stiff and straight, stretching his neck to see over that long bonnet.

Mr. Morgan out in the weather again swinging open his high gate, marching with it through its arc, his rubbers black and shining in the headlights, rain driving into him with wind in his face. The extraordinary things that happened in the dead of night. Every other kid in the district sound asleep, rain thudding down, every other kid snoring his head off, but Perry out driving in the Rolls.

Now pull the other leg, Perry the Cherry, they'd say.

Old Clarrie giving you a ride in his Rolls?

Who you kiddin', Benson?, they'd say.

Water spraying everywhere; Mr. Morgan thudding back into his seat; driving about thirty feet; then heaving himself out into the night once more to shut the gate behind him; the Rolls grumbling and muttering to itself, probably feeling cross at being started up at such an hour, Perry sneaking across a hand to pat the wheel, to stroke it, to take a sudden man-size grip on it.

Perry at the wheel doing a hundred. . . .

I'm coming through, Mum. Brrrrrrr. Out of the way, you lions; jump clear, you elephants, or I'll iron you flat; it's Perry to the rescue at a hundred miles an hour. Can't you hear that siren wailing?

"Hands off, Benson Boy!"

Looking up at Mr. Morgan in surprise.

Mr. Rotten Morgan; why don't you go away? How dare you step into my Rolls? How dare you talk to Mr. Perry Benson Esquire? I'm driving my Rolls and I'll stand no lip from you.

Humming back along the road. Slapping into pot holes. Crack. Wind-tossed night and rain spuming from the windshield. Back to the top of the hill and down the Benson side in next to no time. Ten minutes groping along on foot but only seconds in the Rolls.

Barp. Barp.

Steaming in through the gate like a ship, sounding the horn.

Barp.

Here we are, Mum. Here we come. I did it, Mum. All that way I did it. You didn't think I'd bring the Rolls. Captured it from him, Mum. Got my gun in his ribs. It was a real hard fight but I won.

7
Somebody Else's House

"I see no car, Benson Boy."

"Round the back, Mr. Morgan. Round there. Round there. Farther. In the mud. On the curve. Farther. Mum missed the curve and backed down the hill. Don't stop here. You keep going, Mr. Morgan. You keep going round this curve."

"Could anyone, I ask you, say less in more words?"

"There it is, Mr. Morgan. You stop. You stop here. *Here we are, Mum. Mr. Morgan's brought the Rolls.*"

Little green Morris shining with rain in the light from the Rolls, looking empty, looking marooned, two doors open, back wheels deep almost underground.

"No one in that car, boy. No one there."

"They were, Mr. Morgan. I left them there. True."

"No one in it, boy. House looks shut up too. Been dreaming, boy? Are you sure you were stuck tonight and not some other time?"

But Mr. Morgan stepped down and Perry followed to the ground.

"Are you sure you were not the one who fell and hit his head? Got any lumps there, boy? Lumps or bumbs or holes in the head?" Mr. Morgan picking his way out through lank wet grass. "No one in it, Benson Boy. But I can see that someone's been around. How do you open the hood on these fool things?"

Perry fumbled under the dashboard for the hard loop of wire and sharply tugged as he liked to do at other times for Dad. The lock sprang and Mr. Morgan raised the hood but at once dropped it shut again. "Warm," he said, and lifted Perry bodily from the wet and carried him back to the drive, an odd sensation, because it was Mr. Morgan, the hated Mr. Morgan, a warm human surprise. Hands as big as strong arms. "Did you say your father was uncon-

scious? He can't be now. They must be in the house.
Don't see any lights. Do you? No outside lights at
all."

Hurrying with Mr. Morgan holding to his hand,
Mr. Morgan's flashlight shining to the ground. How
marvelous it was having someone *there*. How could
such an enormous creature be all man? So huge he
broke the weather, sheltered Perry from the rain, so
huge that troubles were getting smaller and smaller
the longer he was around.

Mr. Morgan pacing up the path where Dad had
fallen not so long ago. "Mrs. Benson! Are you
there?"

Perry striding at his side. "She's in there, Mr.
Morgan. There's a lamp alight. See?"

"Lamp? What are you talking about? The electricity hasn't failed."

"We haven't got any electricity here."

"Good Gordon Highlanders, haven't you? I've
heard it said there never was a crankier man." Mr.
Morgan knocking at the door. "Mrs. Benson. Are
you in there? It's Morgan. Clarence Morgan. Your
neighbor from down the road. Shall I come inside
or wait out here? It is my pleasure to be of service,
ma'am."

What a strange thing to say. So nervously he said
it, or that was how it seemed.

Mr. Morgan still knocking at the door, Perry knocking too, but no one coming, no one stirring in there, no sounds except water spilling to the earth from tanks overflowing and leafy branches scraping at walls and wind roaring in big trees along the road. Mr. Morgan made a throaty sound. "Peculiar people you Bensons are. You live here, don't you? Why knock on your own back door? You can go inside, can't you? In you go. Or have you imagined it all? Is it only a night light burning there? Are your parents asleep in bed? If they are I'm going to look a fool. You don't walk in your sleep, do you, boy? But nothing would surprise me. Nothing I say, even though that engine was warm."

"I haven't imagined it, Mr. Morgan. True I haven't."

"Well, in you go then, for pity's sake. It's wet out here. In you go and see."

"Please come too."

"I'm a stranger here."

"I'm inviting you."

"Are you indeed? But what shall I do if the baby's there?"

That great big man, that mountainous man, that bell-tent shaped man looming in the flashlight glow looked so concerned.

"Gee, Mr. Morgan. Babies don't hurt. Babies are little."

The huge man glanced down with a very deep frown.

"They are, Mr. Morgan. True. Only little. Is that why you chain your gate at night? Because you're scared?"

"No doubt about it," Mr. Morgan rumbled. Rumbled like thunder. "You are an extraordinary child. Very well. I shall come in with you. Will you lead?"

But Perry had wanted Mr. Morgan to lead. That was the whole idea. He was the man. Just a little behind, holding Mr. Morgan by the hand, was where Perry had wanted to be. But he drew the door open an inch or two, drew it open grumbling, drew it open shivering. Lots of gloom in there; light in the kitchen; that was all. A lamp on the kitchen table flickering in the draft. Everything else was dark and quiet and empty. Like somebody else's house. No life in there at all. "Mum? Mr. Morgan's here. Mum, he's brought the Rolls. Have you got the baby in there?"

Mr. Morgan was pushing at him. "Go on. In you go. Get inside out of the rain. If the baby's there it'll have to be, I suppose."

But Perry was becoming troubled in an unexpected way. "What is it about babies, Mr. Morgan? About new babies? Are they catching or something? Like the rotten old mumps?"

"No, boy, no."

"My Mum didn't tell me they were catching."

"They're not!"

"Well whatchoo frightened of?"

"I'm not explaining these things to you! Will you get in out of the rain!"

And Perry was put there. Again picked up and somehow put. Like a parcel. The door opened, they were inside, the door closed.

"Mum," Perry bawled, "are you there? Mum, answer me. . . . She's not here, Mr. Morgan. Where's she gone?"

A quiet house, so quiet, so dark except for the kitchen flicker.

"Mrs. Benson," the big man bellowed, "can you hear me? It's Morgan from along the road. Are you in trouble somewhere?" Mr. Morgan shining his flashlight along the passage and over the walls, Mum's oil paintings hanging there and her abstract mobiles contorting silently on hairlike wires. "Great grief," Mr. Morgan said, "what are they?" Fluid shadows of curious kinds on the ceiling. "Not here,"

he said, "Where's she gone? And your father too?
I'm sure we didn't pass them on the road. See if
they've returned to bed. Stranger things have happened. There's a good lad, go along and see. Take
the torch with you. And while you're at it look in
every room. Just in case, you know."

"In case of what, Mr. Morgan?"

"I don't know. Just in case—of course."

"In case of what of course, Mr. Morgan? I'm
scared."

"Nonsense, boy. In your own house? You couldn't
be."

"You're scared, too, aren't you? Sending me on my
own. I thought you were looking after me. You great
big man. Why won't you come with me?"

"Because it's your house, Benson Boy, and it
would not be polite of me, wandering through your
house in the nighttime."

"That's silly, Mr. Morgan. I wouldn't mind."

"Silly it may be. Off you go."

"Don't you run away."

"I could not imagine that I'd be likely to."

I'm not sure of you, Mr. Morgan. What you being
silly for, you stupid old man? What you not telling
me? Scared of a tiny little baby? You're mad.

Perry talking out loud: "Hey, baby, have you

been born? Mr. Morgan's scared of you. It's Perry here. I'm not scared. Don't you jump out and frighten me. Mr. Morgan's come to take us in the Rolls. Hey, Dad, where you hiding? What you people trying to do to me? You're all mad. I hate you."

Perry flashing the light into room after room, talking at the top of his voice all the time, talking all the spooks away. Nothing in his own room either; only wardrobe stuff tumbled on the floor. Nothing in Mum and Dad's room; only bedclothes in disarray. Nothing in the baby's room that had not been there for a month or more; brand new cot and lots of lace, all sorts of fancy things, ribbons and bows and fluffy things. It'd *have* to be a girl—no self-respecting baby boy would last in there a day.

No one anywhere.

Nothing to be scared about.

Perry wrinkling his nose. What a scaredy cat you are, Mr. Morgan. "Hey, Mr. Morgan. No one, see, no babies here."

But the door was slamming shut as if caught on a wind and the big fat man had gone. "Hey, Mr. Morgan. Wait for me."

Perry went wailing down the passage.

"Gee willikens, what you doing to me, all you

people? Everybody disappearing all the time."

Perry crashing open the back door and plunging outside, one foot squarely placed in the middle of a shattering cat dish, mouth open wide for yelling with. "Hey, hey. Don't leave me. Where're you goin', you horrible old man?"

Catching Mr. Morgan in the torchlight only yards away. "Watch your language, boy, or you'll be feeling my hand. And shine that light off my eyes. Here, give it to me. Can you see a horse? I'd swear I heard a draft horse neigh. Has that crazy father of yours still got a working horse in this day and age?"

Mr. Morgan shining the light down the path to the shed where the little Morris had been, shining on past the shed down the green hill, the raining hill.

"Great Caesar's ghost! He has!"

Mum and Dad together. There they were. Staggering a bit. Holding each other up. Looking as if they had been dunked in the dam, the muddy red dam. Mum and Dad together struggling into view, trying to drag Joe, trying to lead him by the nose. Joe not wanting to come. Joe never liked work even in the bright light of noon. Joe only liked to play. Tossing his head and whinnying as if to say, "Get lost, will you? Waking me up at three. What's the lark?

What's the big idea? It's raining. Horses have got rights. Hadn't you heard?"

Perry stood back a step, a step *away* from the troublesome present.

Maybe it is a dream. Maybe it's got to be. Maybe it's raining though. Cats and dogs and blowing a gale. Maybe the roof's lifted off and water's pouring all over me bed. Maybe I'm lying there getting soaked through and through.

Mr. Morgan, that enormous man, was lumbering down the path toward Mum and Dad. "You don't need the horse," he was bellowing. "Let the poor brute go."

8
Fairy Tales
and Legends Stuff

It was a grown-up's world again and Perry was looking on. He supposed. There was always a chance that something spooky was happening. Fairy tales and legends stuff. Perhaps like Alice he had stepped through a mirror! And things were getting more and more out of hand. Perhaps in a minute horses really would start talking. Having a doubt about whether you were sound asleep or wide awake was kind of rare.

So he trailed after Mr. Morgan, or what he took to be Mr. Morgan, following him down the raining hill toward what he took to be Mum and Dad and whinnying old Joe. Slop, slop, through the wet. Talk about wet. It was like taking a shower. Except that he hadn't soaped himself. Or shampooed his hair. Or taken his clothes off. Or stuck his toe down the plug hole as he had a compulsive habit of doing to the hysterical displeasure of Dad. There was a memory of Dad screaming, "What does one do with a kid who keeps on sticking his toe down a hole that's concreted in the ground? One of these days we'll not get it out again. One of these days he'll be clanking round the earth dragging Australia with him by the toe."

As if anyone could!

That was Dad all over, always taking things too far. Dad enjoyed having his hysterics. He was terrific. No day was complete without a performance. Mum used to laugh and laugh but there were times when Dad couldn't see the funny side. Any more than he saw the funny side now. "Who are you?" Dad was yelling, peering into the light, rubbing at his eyes, leaning on his horse to prop himself up, and looking very woolly and wild, sometimes reaching for his head and moaning between words, but yelling just the same. "Who's there? Who's dazzling me? Who's telling me what to do?"

"It's Morgan here."

"Morgan?" yelled Dad. "From up the hill and over the top and down the other side? That Morgan?

That political anachronism? What's he doing on my land? You gird your loins, Mister, you anoint your head, you get to blazes out of here."

Mum was pleading. "No, Denis. No, dear. We asked him to come. We needed him. We went to him. It's Perry who brought him here."

And Perry was trying to get a word in edgewise, a very important word. "The baby, Mum? Have we got it yet or have we still got to go?" But no one heard.

"You mean Perry?" Dad went on yelling, wincing from pain. "Perry our boy? What's he got to do with it? Perry going to Morgan! *Our* Perry calling on Morgan! Our Perry bringing that capitalist here? We need Morgan like we need the plague."

"Sink me," bellowed Mr. Morgan, "you can see where the poor child gets it from."

"Mum, I wish you'd listen. I wish you'd hear. It's me. It's Perry. He's brought the Rolls to take you to hospital. Do we still have to go? Has our baby been born?"

"Go to hospital in the Rolls?" yelled Dad. "Not so-and-so likely! We go nowhere with him. Everywhere we go we paddle our own canoe. Be hanged to you, Mr. Moneybags. Coming in here ordering me around. Shining lights in my eyes. On my own bit of land."

"It's his head," Mum cried. "He's not himself, as you can see. Will you leave the arrangements to me, Denis dear? There are matters of greater urgency than pride."

"Don't apologize for me, woman. On my own land. Apologizing for me. I'll not have it, understand?"

Perry tried shouting. "Is the baby born yet? Gee willikens. It's me. It's Perry. Look. Here. See. Me."

"Oh, Mr. Morgan, he doesn't mean it. He's had such a terrible blow. Got such a lump. He's not himself."

"He's not?" Mr. Morgan bellowed. "Well, you could have fooled me. The radical. The rat bag. If it were not for your gracious self, ma'am, wild elephants would not have dragged me here."

"Hey, you people! Hey, hey! Isn't anybody going to listen to me? Aren't we supposed to be having a baby? Aren't we?"

More and more it was like the world behind the mirror where everything had to be upside down or back-to-front or not there at all. What was in the mirror when you were looking the other way? Things you'd never dream of? Gee willikens. So what went on in the middle of the night when you were dead to the world in bed? Kids getting their wits scared out of them but never brave enough to *tell* afterward which was why you never heard? People being nocturnal like cats and possums and screech owls? Like Mum blinking past the glare issuing from Mr. Morgan's hand. Things like Dad taking a swing at Joe's flank and snarling, "Come on, horse. Useless horse. Fat horse. Shift yourself. Earn your keep." Mum shrilling, "Perry? Is that Perry there? What's that you say, Perry?"

"I've been saying lots of things."

"Have you, dear? Have you, dear? So have we. So much on our minds."

Mr. Morgan booming again like a great bass drum. "Look here, Benson, even if you *have* been hit on the head you can't expect the horse to get you there. You'd have had to start off yesterday."

"I'm pulling my car out, if you don't mind, Morgan! Am I answerable for my own actions on my own land? And I'll not be responsible if you don't stand aside. If he kicks, if he bites, the bad luck's yours."

Big Joe flopping and squelching in the wet, showing his teeth, flicking his tail, looking good and mad as Joe always did when he got the message that work was around.

"Benson, you're too sick to drive a car."

"You heard me, Morgan. Don't stand in front of

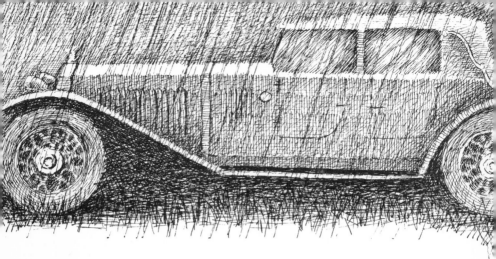

my horse. He's a nasty bit of work when he's roused."

Everybody floundering in the wet, everybody trying to get out of everybody's way, with Perry raising his cry of bewilderment. "What's wrong with all you people? Shouting at each other all the time. What about our baby? Isn't anybody ever going to tell me?"

"Oh Perry, Perry, of course we haven't got it yet. Surely you know." Mum's hand came down out of nowhere and held him as if at last he belonged to someone and all his troubles flooded back at her.

"Well, what are you arguing at each other for? I thought we were in a hurry."

"We are in a hurry, dear."

"I thought that was why I had to run to Mr. Morgan's. All on my own. In the dark. All that way."

"Yes, dear, that's true. No one has deceived you."

"Well, whatchoo shouting at each other for?"

"Perry, you're shouting, too."

And somehow they were making their way along the drive, Joe's trailing harness clinking on the stones. There stood the regal Rolls, washed gleaming by rain, exhaust smoke drifting from the stern. And down in the mud stood the Morris, like a rowboat stuck in sand.

"Everyone's overwrought, Perry," Mum said. "It happens to grown-ups as well as to boys and girls."

"But Mr. Morgan's brought his car. Can't you see? Cranked it up by hand. Chucked out all the boxes.

Brushed out all the spiders. Cranked it up and all."

"Yes, darling, I can see. But I think your father wants to handle it alone. You must try to understand. Your father likes to do things on his own. He's a proud man. Mr. Morgan understands, I'm sure."

"Do I, ma'am?"

"Of course you do. Your sense of humor saves the day. Tomorrow, Perry, your father will laugh, too."

Mum was standing in the light from the Rolls looking down at Dad staggering to hold Joe in check and underneath hitch a chain to the chassis of the car. Mum's face was clearly seen, unhappily regarding Dad. Something wasn't right down there. Perry did not care for it and wanted to shut his eyes. Dad, on his own, slithering around.

"My husband," Mum said, "as you can see, delights in doing every little thing in the only difficult way. It builds character, he says. If it gives us ulcers, who cares?" That wasn't loyal of Mum, coming out with that when Mr. Morgan was around, repeating things she said at other times when she was cross with Dad. Though what ulcers were, Perry couldn't say. Perhaps, like warts, they broke out on your hands. Mum standing there with a gray face, streaming wet with rain, set and gray and lined, suddenly making Perry mad.

"I'm going to help him," he cried. "It's not fair. He hit his head on a stone."

But a huge hand held Perry back by the arm. "Don't interfere. Do you want to be kicked by the horse? Leave your father be. You're only a little boy." Perry tried to fight clear but it was like being nailed to a wooden frame. "You did send this lad to me, ma'am, I suppose? He didn't come of his own accord?"

"I sent him."

"It was a long way for a little boy."

"I'm not little," Perry screeched. "You take your hands off me."

"He was very brave."

And there was Dad swaying in the mud, mud on his face, mud in his hair, as if at any moment he might fall, but he had chained Big Joe to the car.

"Good on you, Dad," Perry shrilled, "good on you, Dad." And his shoulder was suddenly free. The big fat man's big fat hand had gone.

"Good night, ma'am."

Mr. Morgan was stepping away, stepping up into the Rolls, slamming his door, and Dad was slapping Big Joe on the side. "Get up there, Joe. Get up there, Joe. *Pull, Joe.*"

Joe pulled and Mr. Morgan reversed past the curve of the drive.

Joe pulled and the chain unwound and trailed through the mud and the Morris didn't move and everything suddenly was black and wet, and Joe, it seemed, kicked up his heels and clanking his chain like a graveyard ghost thudded invisibly into the paddocks below where early peas were sown, great hoofs thrusting the seeds deep underground.

"Oh, Denis," Mum cried, "you didn't properly secure the chain."

Where was Dad? Was he running after Joe? Where was everybody? There was nothing to see and the lights of the Rolls had become a glow in the trees too far gone to pursue.

"Mum," yelled Perry. "Mum. . . . He's gone. . . . Why did you let him go?"

"Because he couldn't stay." Mum's voice was heavy, as if she carried a heavy load. "I don't expect a boy to understand."

"I went all that way for nothing?"

"Yes, dear."

"On my own."

Mum found him and held him and Dad's voice, thick and hoarse, was somewhere near. "I've made a mess of things. Do I ever make anything else? Oh, my head. Oh, my God. Is our baby coming, love, or have we still a little time?"

"Come here, Denis," Mum said. "Can you see me? Give me your hand."

Dad came shuffling up. Dad came and joined. Dad and Mum and Perry in the raining blackness on the drive.

"It would have been better, wouldn't it, if I hadn't come round? If I'd stayed out dead to the world. You were doing all right, you and the boy. But I've got to stick my nose in. I've got to say be hanged to old Moneybags Morgan; we do things like having our family on our own. I know he was only being kind. And he must have been scared stiff, poor old man. What an effort it must have been. Never having had a kid of his own. And I've given him a horrid time all these years. Poor old devil dragged in by the hair when a baby is about to be born. . . ."

Mum wasn't saying a thing except that her hold on Perry was incredibly tight and she might have been moaning but he wasn't sure.

But Dad was talking all the time.

"That horse'll not go back to the yard. I'll not be catching him now. It'll be daylight, daylight before I get near him. We're up the creek, love. We'll be bringing this baby into the world on our own. How's that for a funny story? Back to nature, the way I've always wanted it. Can't you hear those gods laughing fit to split their sides? If you stick your neck out far enough you get it chopped off every time. But having a baby is a natural thing; it shouldn't terrify a man. . . ."

Mum was breathing deeply, deep breaths, prodigious breaths, but still not saying a word. Worrying Perry.

So many things that happened in the grown-up world seemed to have nothing to do with a boy but they came flowing over just the same.

No good these grown-ups saying you don't understand or won't understand or it's grown-up business and not your concern when the rain was blowing a storm and Mum and Dad were hanging together and you were getting smothered in the middle of them. Though it was hard trying to work out why God should be laughing. Hadn't they been saying their prayers?

Mum in a peculiar voice was urging Dad, "Let's go back to the house. Let's do it now. Bring the suitcase with you, dear. You'll have to get it from the car."

The oddness of her voice must have frightened Dad because he broke away into the blackness, probably downhill to the car, calling, "Wait here, wait there. Oh my God. The things that happen to me. What does a man do? I mean. . . ."

"Perry," Mum was saying, "make your way up to the house. Be as quick as you can. Stuff some paper and kindling wood into the stove. Put a match to it and open the flue to make it roar. Fill the iron kettle and the big black pot and bring them to the boil. No time to lose. While you're waiting on the water light all the lamps you can find. Be careful with the matches, dear. My strong son. My brave boy."

Mum was still clinging to him as if she needed him there to help her to stand, but she pushed him away.

"Go now, Perry."

9
Pillar of Fire

There was a noise in Perry's head like wind whistling through a crack, fading in and fading out. It lay underneath his thoughts and somehow disconnected his head from the rest of himself.

A strange, squeamish feeling it was, like suddenly having grown to a great height with arms and hands left way down underneath almost out of touch. As if everything happening was happening at a distance. The paper crackling in his hands might have been crackling yesterday and the match flaring might have been a match he struck a year ago. It was weird. But the paper caught alight and he pushed handfuls of kindling from the wood cupboard in on top of it and flames came leaping back at him out of the fire box doors; real flames and real smoke and the burning smell of real gum tree sticks.

Mum and Dad crashed in through the back door; or that was how it sounded, as if they had crashed bodily through the panel without first bothering to open it; then went crashing on down the passage as if repeatedly striking the walls on either side. Fire roared, as it rarely did, in the large black stove, air and fire roared through it sounding like a furnace in the flue. Big Joe whinnied from somewhere close to the house, as if laughing his silly-looking head off, which he probably was. Dad yelled, "Can you bring more light?" Perry struck matches to light candles jammed into the mouths of wax-encrusted bottles. "Are you bringing more light?" Dad was beginning to sound impatient as if seconds were important.

Mum had her suitcase open and by candlelight was arranging on her dressing table things she had bought from the chemist's shop. Dad was pacing back and forth talking to himself, saying, "I don't know, I don't know," or something like that and Mum said, "Put the candles here, Perry, but I'd rather you brought the lamps." Mum went on arranging things on her dressing table with jerky movements like a puppet.

Perry, almost mimicking her actions, went jerking

round the house hunting for lamps, striking matches everywhere, and sounds of Dad seemed to be coming from every room in turn, Dad everywhere talking to himself, shedding his muddy clothes, as Perry was trying to do, washing himself in the bathroom and thudding up and down with towels and sheets and bowls and numerous articles of no immediate use—or so Mum said—once stopping his breathless rush loudly to complain, "Haven't we got a book about it?"

"About what, dear?" Mum must have asked.

"About delivering babies. It's stupid not having a book about it. I can't understand why we haven't got a book about it. We've got books about everything else."

"You don't need a book about it, dear."

"You speak for yourself. All you've got to do is have it. Women are having babies all the time. Night and day. All the time. But men get mixed up in it hardly ever." Dad had something like a sob in his voice. "I don't know anything about babies. So help me bob, I'm thirty-eight and we've only had one kid before. It's no good hiding our heads in the sand, love. When that baby starts coming I'll faint, I think; I'll start running, I think. I've got to be the midwife, haven't I? Or whatever it is you call it. I have to spank it on the bottom to make it breathe. I have to cut the cord and tie it. I have to bind it up in swaddling clothes, don't I, or is that in the Bible? I'm telling you, I—don't—know—what—to do. I'll break it. I'll drop it. I don't know how you can lie there being so calm. This is the most terrible thing that has happened to me."

"That's right, Perry," Mum said, "put the lamps around and take the candles away. That's a good boy. Put a candle in the bathroom and another in the kitchen. Wherever you find a dark spot put a candle, please. When our baby starts coming Dad is going to run away and one fall is enough for one night. I want you to take particular care to light his way."

"For Heaven's sake," Dad grumbled, "what a thing to say. He'll think you mean it."

Mum was lying on top of the bed covered by a sheet, breathing very deeply as she had done outside on the drive, but now gripping with each straining hand at the bedrail behind her head. Mum seemed suddenly to have been seized by pain, to have become unnaturally white, seemed actually to be biting on her lips as if she might bite them through and to be silencing a cry that should have welled out of her, that she should never have tried to fight down.

But Dad enveloped Perry, obstructing his startled view.

"Perry," Dad said, "is the water ready?"

"Dad, it hurts her."

"That's right, son."

"It hurts her."

"When you were born. When I was born. For every baby ever born."

That's what Dad said and Perry to his surprise was confronted by the blank face of a door. Somehow he had been transported bodily and shut out as if he had never been in there at all and everything he had seen had happened perhaps a year or longer ago or had been imagined for an instant only in his mind. So suddenly had Mum's face turned into the face of a door. He'd been *manhandled* again and his temper flared and his first pounded on that door, but Dad's voice came back with authority from the other side.

"Go away!"

"No!"

"I asked about the water, didn't I? Go and see. Be a help to us."

"I suppose runnin' all that way to Mr. Morgan's wasn't helpin' you? I suppose doin' all those things for Mum wasn't helpin' you?"

"I suppose leaving your billy-cart on the path was helping us no end."

That was like a bucketful of something sodden and cold emptying all over him.

"Bring the water," the voice said.

"How is it I can mess about with the stove tonight and not any other time?"

"Perry, do as you're told!"

"How is it you're always tellin' me I'll get scalded if I touch boiling water, but you're not tellin' me now?"

The door opened so swiftly that air was sucked with it into the room.

Dad's face appeared like a picture in a tall frame. Dad with his teeth bared and his sleeves rolled up and his hair standing on end, giving Perry such a fright that he stumbled against the wall.

"I'll tell you something, Perry Benson," Dad said. "In every story I've read and every film I've seen, babies being born and kettles of water go hand in hand. Now you can make of that whatever you choose. Like pepper and salt they go hand in hand. So I need water for something! So," Dad yelled, "will you bring water here!" Then Mum gave a long cry as if trying to attract the attention of someone living half a mile away and Dad's hair stood up straighter than before and Perry fled for the kitchen wailing aloud, "Poor little baby. Fancy gettin' born into this family. If you've got time to change your mind, baby, you change it now. You go somewhere else, baby, while you've got time. It's only crazy people who live here."

Water was hissing and spitting everywhere, squirting out of the spout of the iron kettle, spilling over the sides of the big black pot, sizzling and jumping and steaming and clanging on the hot plate, steam everywhere, the place smelling hot and wet and scorched like Mum's laundry on washing day, only worse, as if everything were a moment short of blowing up like a thunderclap. And that would be wonderful. Oh, that would be marvelous. If the stove blew up now! Boom. A dirty great hole in the kitchen wall. Boom. Maybe half the roof of the house off. Boom. Mum having the baby in the bedroom with Dad holding an umbrella to keep off the rain. Except that they didn't have an umbrella. Boom. Perry floating round in orbit with angel wings playing the Jew's harp.

"Dad," he bawled, "I can't touch the stove. It's too hot. It's going too hard. The rotten old thing's going to blow up. Mum shouldn't have told me to open the flue. It's on fire, I'll betcha. I'll betcha it's on fire." And Perry went rushing to the back door out into the rain and sure enough it was, the flue pipe blazing like a blow torch, smoke and fire and

sparks pouring into the night, lighting up everything for a hundred yards around.

"Oh my," Perry wailed, "we're on fire. We really are. Oh, gee willikens. Fire, fire. How can we be on fire in the rain?"

He went flying back into the house, up the passage to the bedroom door. Bang, bang on the door. "Dad!" Bang on the door again. *"Dad, Dad, we're on fire."*

"That's fine. Put the water on then. Bring it to the boil as quickly as you can."

"Dad, Dad, the house'll burn down."

"Jolly good. That's the style."

"Dad, Dad, you've got to come."

"The things that happen to a man. Oh, for crying out loud. Never in a million years!"

"Dad, you're not listening to me."

"Where's the water I asked for? You're taking your time, or have you left it at the door?"

That stupid man hadn't heard a word.

"Can't you hear me in there?" Perry shrilled. "Don't you know what I'm sayin'?"

He banged again at the door and rattled at the knob but Dad must have turned the key.

"We'll all burn to death if we don't get outa here. Dad! Dad!"

"I'll open the window later. Run along, Perry. Put the kettle on for a cup of tea. They tell me they like a cup of tea afterward."

He was crackers, he was crazy, that stupid father man.

Perry rushed to the kitchen and the whole place was roaring and shaking. The flue was going woof-woof and beating itself against the inside of the chimney. The kettle and the pot were boiling over everywhere; squirts and spouts of steam and even worse were the smells of scorching wood and red-hot iron.

"Stop it, stop it, stop it, you terrible stove! What am I to do with you?" But screaming and jumping and shaking angry fists made no difference to it at all.

Again outside into the rain, Perry leaping beyond the step as if already it had turned to coals that might burn through the soles of his shoes, and there overhead still cracked the pillar of fire like a giant Roman candle, lighting up the shed and the hydrangeas and the ferns and the plowed earth and the rain and a lot of stupid birds who went dashing hither and thither thinking it was getting-up time.

"It's awful, awful, awful, all the things that'll burn. All the pictures Mum's painted, all the furniture Dad's made, *all my house,* just because some stupid baby won't wait to get born."

Everywhere flames leaping and licking and crackling and roaring. That's how it would be. A horrible rending sound, all the walls folding up one on top of the other shooting out sparks and explosions. Nothing left but a little heap of ashes. That's how it would be. Perry living on his own. Poor little orphan boy. Perry living in a hollow log deep in the bush sharing with possums and parrots. No one to cook gem-scones with honey.

Frenziedly banging on the bedroom door. "It's firing out here. Aren't you goin' to listen to me? What we wastin' our time with that stupid baby for?"

"Perry. Go away."

10
Flowers Coming Up All Around

So Perry broke down the door with his bare fists and tucked his mother under one arm and his father under the other and carried them kicking to safety, and when he reached the back door he kneed it open and with a flick of each hip tossed each protesting parent into the rain where the fire could not harm them. But he didn't really; he stood in the passage doing nothing, wondering what it could be that a boy could do when his father cared so little and his mother answered never. So he sprang madly high into the ceiling, as high as Dad had climbed on the step ladder, and dragged Mum's mobiles down clattering and clanging and tore her pictures from the walls and gathered up Dad's chairs and little round tables and chests studded with copper nails and

transported them all to the door which he kneed
open before tossing the lot in one gigantic armful
into the rain where fire could not consume them.
But he didn't do that either, except in his imagin-
ings, and the back door swung open and in came the
giant all wet and black and shining and huge, beating his chest and booming fe, fi, fo, fum.

"You crazy Bensons," the giant bellowed, "I
thought signal fires went out with George III. Why
don't you crazy people install the telephone!" And
he came farther in, shaking the house with his footsteps, booming into the kitchen where Perry could
not see him. "I've struck some chimney fires in my
time but you've got yourselves a ripper here. Hasn't
anyone the brains to shut off the draft and close the
flue? Why don't you people cook with electricity! Or
eat everything raw! You're not safe to let out in the
rain."

That was what the giant said, or something like it.
Or was it fe, fi, fo, fum? But when did he say it: an
hour ago, or now? Time was difficult to follow in this
odd world that happened when a fellow should have
been asleep in bed, completely asleep, and warm,
but was leaning like something almost dead against a
wall, as if in the act of his falling the wall had got in
his way. Then like an overhanging cloud the giant

came. So huge he was. So huge. He could have crushed Perry's life between the fingers of a hand, but he lifted Perry from his knees and gently held him and in silence stood with him beneath the mobiles drifting in the gloom, beneath the sound of rain on roofing iron and a cry like Mum in awful pain.

"Ah!" the giant said, as if he felt the pain. "Your mother's in there." Choked, the giant sounded, as if the pain took his breath away. Great arms seemed to crush Perry, seemed to lift him to a height as if by some ghastly change of fortune he was about to be dashed to the ground, but he was swept into a kitchen chair at a table set for breakfast hours ago by Mum. Set last night or last year? Oh dear, oh dear. In a kitchen that had billowed and belched with steam but was so quiet now. Things smelled hot, smelled steamed, but nothing had turned into heaps of ashes. Nothing rattled or roared any more. When *had* that giant walked in at the door shaking the floor with his footsteps and the house had been poised at the brink of going *boooom*?

"Poor little baby," the giant said, "getting born." Then he started making a pot of tea, confidently, as if everything in Mum's kitchen was placed exactly as it was in his own.

"Didn't that horse shift the car?" the giant said. "Miserable old nag. I thought he had the look in his eye. So I reckoned to wait at my gate until you went by. You didn't, Benson Boy. But you sent up a signal that should have brought the Fire Brigade. They must be sleeping tonight, very soundly, that Fire Brigade. How could *anyone* sleep when such things are happening to you? But they do, boy, they do."

He was talking louder now, that giant was, louder than he needed to, and his movements round the kitchen were on the jerky side, the way that Mum's had been. Cups he put out, tea he poured. "With milk? Sugar, I suppose? How many spoons? I hope that father of yours shows more sense in there than he showed outside."

Mum was yelling underneath Mr. Morgan's trumpeting sounds. The noise that man made clattering round the kitchen! But Mum had a good pair of lungs. She was louder still.

"God bless me heart and soul," the giant said. "Isn't it enough to wake the dead!" And started gulping mightily at his tea in between his shouting and his clattering round. So hot the tea it was a wonder he didn't burst into flame. His mouth must have been cast from solid iron. Much too hot for Perry's tongue.

"Don't worry, boy," the giant said. "Be calm, keep cool. There's nothing to it, I assure you. Ladies are having babies every day. They have to, or there wouldn't be a soul around."

Perry complained, "It's me tongue. . . ."

Clatter, crash, bang, the giant went, charging here and there, getting noisier and jerkier by the minute. A terrible act he was putting on, almost as bad as Dad. Spilling his tea he was and breaking out in a sweat across his brow.

"I've burned me tongue. . . ."

"Imagine some poor woman giving birth to me," the giant said, "but she did, you know, seventy-one years ago come next November 3. Sort of proving it, don't you see? Nothing to it. Of course I was smaller at the time. No need to get excited about it, boy."

"I've burned my tongue."

"Your mother's singing, really. Sheer joy for the love of living. Just a little out of tune."

Pacing back and forth the giant was, mopping at his sweat, scratching at his head, looking *scared*, and trying his hardest not to hear the slightest sound that he didn't make himself. Even Perry knew that, and if ever Perry had felt like nothing much at all it was now.

But Mr. Morgan was standing still, as if every

nerve had been arrested by command. And there wasn't a sound, not even from Mum, nor from the wind or rain. A stillness had come.

"What's that you say, Benson Boy?"

"I've burned my tongue."

"Or wasn't it you? I think it might have been a cry. The kind a baby makes when it's born. . . ."

That giant. That huge man. He had tears in his eyes. The sissy man. "Well I never," he said. "What *do* you know. Bless my heart and soul. What a sound I've heard today. Thank you," the giant said, "for having me catch my breath at the first squeak a new life made. Seventy-one I am and never heard the like of it before." His hand raised Perry. "It's a miracle we have here. Let's go see."

Peculiar people these grown-ups were, the mysteries their words made. "I thought you said it was happening all the time," Perry squealed. "I thought you said babies being born was nothing."

"That's true. Nothing much. Like flowers coming up all around they're happening every day. Millions of them you never know about and never see. Do you think they'd mind if we crept in, boy, quietly?"

"I dunno. Well, I don't, do I? We'll have to take the water if we go."

"What water is that, boy?"

"Mum said when babies were being born you always put the kettle on."

"You do?"

"That's what she said."

"When did she say this?"

"Before. And Dad asked me to make a pot of tea because afterward they always have one."

Mr. Morgan looked confused. "Who do?"

"The babies, I suppose."

"You don't give babies pots of tea."

"That's what he said."

"Good grief. . . . Very well, let's take water with us. Let's take tea. Let's take it all. Go along, boy. Knock on the door. See if they'll mind."

But Perry didn't move.

"Run along, Benson Boy. Knock on the door. It's your house and family."

"If it's catching I don't want to get it."

Poor giant, creasing his brow. "Now what bridge have we crossed? You don't want to get what?"

"Whatever it is that new babies have got."

The giant's voice went up the scale in a most ungiantlike way. "New babies haven't *got* anything. I told you that before. They're purer than the driven snow."

"Well, what are you scared for?"

"I—am—not—scared. But I *am* a bachelor and not accustomed to these things."

"Nor am I."

"Nor are you what?"

"Accustomed to these things."

Mr. Morgan sighed deeply. "Very well. Together we shall go. But you're pushing your luck, Benson Boy. I've yet to make my mind up about you."

What was that supposed to mean?

But Perry's giant was not a giant any more. Not ten feet tall any more. Perhaps down to six feet and steadily shrinking as might have happened in a dream. Perhaps, in the end, before the dream burst, he would turn into a puddle and trickle out through a crack in the floor. Then Perry would waken a second time with the storm blustering at his window pane, and blowing into his room, with a rainsoaked pillow and puddles round his head, and everything would start all over again but take a different course.

Mum's bedroom door.

Dad in his shirtsleeves, hair in strands, Dad looking as though he had fallen from a tree, waiting as if he had opened the door to callers he could not see. Dad with a very strange expression, his eyes catching the yellow light from the lamp flickering on the wall, a deeply perturbed look as if there were too many questions with answers he could not find.

Mr. Morgan's big fat hand on Perry's shoulder became so tight that Perry winced from the hurt and shock of it.

"My God, Benson, is the baby *dead?*"

Dad seemed to be as startled by the word as if someone had hit him. "No, no. . . . We'll have to call her Storm. . . . Oh, Morgan. . . . What wonders I have witnessed. Come in, come in. Be the first."

Mum. She looked bedraggled, as if she'd been upended in a barrel; that was how. Oh, Mum. As pale as ever she had been. Paler than that. With tears and slow little smiles and half-stifled sighs and bloodshot eyes and arms limply outstretched, exhausted arms, exhausted fingers. Mum not knowing, really, that anyone was there. Beside her a strange, scrawny, stringly little red object. Perry's jaw fell open.

"Yes, Morgan, a girl. That's all she's asked so far; is it well, is it a girl?"

"Dad," Perry shrilled, "is that it?"

"Shhh," Dad said. "You've brought my water, Morgan. Good. I think we wash her. Isn't she a lovely child? Though I have a feeling we should bathe her in oil. Do you know?"

Thick as thieves they were, like Sunday-best pals. As if Dad had never called Mr. Morgan a miserable

so-and-so or Old Moneybags or those other words that boys were not supposed to know. Patting each other they were. Standing with hands on hips, swaying together, talking about whether you should add hot water to cold or cold water to hot as if they'd been dying to discuss it for years. And were baby soaps really for babies or was that just another trick to deceive the peasantry? Or should they wrap the baby up exactly as it was and head for hospital lickety-spit?

"Septicaemia," Dad was saying, "and all that sort of thing. Infection can happen, can't it? I've had to work with such limited means."

Dad was looking smug now, wearing a slight smile, the casual look, as if delivering babies was something he did every other morning before breakfast along with a few push-ups and a run around the paddock. As if presenting a fellow with an object like *that* and calling it a girl was a great achievement. Gee willikens. Had he stopped to *look* at it?

"Perry."

It was Mum, raising her head an inch or two. "Is that tea? That couldn't be tea? Have you really brought a pot of tea? My clever son. Whatever made you think of it? Come on round the side with it and tell me what you've been doing."

"I've burned my tongue and no one cares."

"Don't they, darling? Goodness me. Well, bring it here and let me see. Did you dream that the night was going to end this way; a beautiful sister in the family?"

"Eh?"

"Isn't she lovely?"

There seemed to be only one answer for that; he poked out his tongue for Mum to inspect.

"Put your tongue in, Perry," Dad said. "What an extraordinary way to address your mother. Are you going to pour her a cup of tea or aren't you? And I could do with one myself. Then I want you to get round the house and extinguish the lights. We're leaving for the hospital immediately. You've got to pull your weight."

"Strike me," Perry shrilled. "Haven't I already?"

Mum shook her head. "Don't be cheeky, darling," she whispered. "Your father's had a trying experience."

"I thought *you* had the baby."

But Mum lifted a tired finger. "Only in a manner of speaking."

"My, my," Mr. Morgan sighed. "A newborn baby. A *new*born baby. Oh, what a sight to see. The life stream. Tonight its wave breaks over me. Thank you, dear Bensons, for allowing me to share in your miracle."

"Come, come," Dad said.

"You have earned my respect, Benson. I don't know how you can be so calm. In your shoes I would have died."

"One rises to the occasion," Dad said. "It's nothing. You would have done the same."

Perry's lips grew rounder and rounder as if a whistle might start sounding there.

"Run along, Perry," Mum said, "and extinguish the lights as your father told you to do. In a minute we'll go."

"Then sit yourself in the car, son, and wait out there."

"In what car?" Perry asked sullenly.

"Why," Mr. Morgan said, "in mine, naturally."

"In the Rolls," Dad said. "Naturally. Ha ha."

11
The Fastest Bowler
in the World

Sitting in the Rolls.

At the wheel.

Sitting up straight and peering out over the long hood. Brrr-rrr. Coming down the hill from Upwey into Fern Tree Gulley at seventy miles an hour. Brrr-rrr-rrr. Watch the curve, Perry. Don't swing out wide. Swing out too far, Perry, and you'll be in the railway cutting fighting with a train.

Mr. Morgan's torchlight was flooding the sparkling drive. Wet gravel sparkling like jewels. A drive made of rubies and amethysts and pearls. Liquid diamonds dripping from trees. In the torchlight came Dad *carrying* Mum with deliberate, heavy strides, Dad planting each foot down flat and wide as if intending never to raise it again. Grotesquely slap,

slap, slap along the sparkling drive to the door of the
Rolls. Veins standing out on his head. Wow. It was a
wonder he didn't blow a valve. *And Mum was carrying the baby,* wrapped like an Eskimo.

"Yes," Mr. Morgan said, "in the back. Heave her
up, man. Plenty of room. Help yourself a little, Mrs.
Benson. That's the idea. Where's that boy?"

Perry sniffed disdainfully. It was a wonder anyone
heard him, the way Dad was puffing and blowing,
but Mum said, "Don't sniff, Perry; use your hand-
kerchief."

Wouldn't it give a fellow the screams!

"He's there?" Mr. Morgan exclaimed. "So he is!
He'll have to grow. Superphosphates are good, I'm
told. Ha ha. Have we got everything? Nothing left
behind? Got the baby, I suppose? I won't keep you a
moment; I feel I ought to check your kitchen stove.
Are you comfortable, ma'am? Put your head on your
husband's shoulder. That's the idea. It's a long time
since a pretty woman was sitting there. . . ."

It was sickening when you remembered all the
muck they'd been slinging at each other for years,
particularly on election days, outside the polling
booth, Dad handing out the cards for one party, Mr.
Morgan handing them out for the other. But Dad
wasn't uttering a sound right now, except puff and
blow. "Denis," Mum was saying, "you shouldn't

have carried me. You're not well. You had that terrible fall."

"Puff, puff," went Dad, though not exactly in words.

"If you've hurt yourself how do you think I'll feel?"

"Puff, puff," went Dad.

"You're a very silly man, but you would insist. It was much too much for you to do."

"It wasn't. Keep your voice down. He's coming back. He'll hear."

"That's all you were trying to do. Trying to impress him. You don't need to impress anybody for my sake. If you've done yourself an injury you have yourself to blame."

Mr. Morgan had come back to the Rolls and was taking a mighty swing at the starting handle. An incredible swing. As if he had more horsepower under his hat than the car had on the road.

"Let it drop, will you?" moaned Dad.

"But I was thrilled," Mum said, "just the same."

"Were you, darling," cried Dad, "were you really?" And kissed her. You could hear the smack from the front seat even with the engine going. It was sickening, *absolutely*.

In leaped Mr. Morgan to take the wheel, all seventy-one years of him, all two hundred and fifty pounds. Crunch. Almost broke the springs. Almost cracked the chassis. Talk about playing to the gallery. If a kid had behaved that way he'd have been told to grow up. "Away we go," Mr. Morgan boomed. "Ha ha." And in reverse drove magnificently backward round the curve of the drive and out through the gateway, dead center, as if he had negotiated it a thousand times before. "Fern Tree Gully Hospital," Mr. Morgan boomed, "here we come. Benson's Home Delivery Service. Ha ha. With the Baby of the Year."

Up the hill they went, Mr. Morgan singing to himself. "Dum-te-dum-te-dum-te-dum." No tune at all. Terrible. Headlights shining on glistening trees, the world out there so sparkling new it could have been made only minutes before. Air so clean. Greens so green. Blacks so black.

"That name, Benson. Storm. Are you really going to call her by it? The wind hasn't blown and the rain hasn't rained, not since she arrived."

"Time will tell, Morgan old friend. Perhaps we could call her Morgana."

"The name is decided," said Mum.

"Is it?" grumbled Dad. "That's news to me."

"It's Denise," Mum said, "in honor of you."

Dad made laughing noises and Perry with a

grimace stretched his neck higher to see better over the hood. Not doing seventy as hoped for, but building up to thirty, every bit of it.

"Dum-te-dum-te-dum-te-dum."

"Hey," shrilled Perry. "Hey, hey. Look there. A red light flashing coming our way."

"Not *coming*, boy," Mr. Morgan boomed, "*arrived* at my gate, I'd say, or I'm no judge of distance. And it's the Fire Brigade or I'm stone blind."

"Fire Brigade?" called Dad. "That rings a bell with me. Has something been on fire round here or have I dreamed it all?"

"You didn't dream it, man, no sir, but young Perry here and I, we took care of it, didn't we, boy?"

"Fire?" cried Mum.

"That chimney of yours, going like a bomb, ma'am. But no harm's done. And get an eyeful of these characters here. . . . All right," he yelled out through the side, "keep your long hair on, you long-haired lot. When your brakes are fifty years old you'll not be stopping in a yard or two either."

Running alongside they were, waving their little hatchets, jumping up and down.

"Hey, Mr. Morgan, you."

"Hey, there, stop your car."

"Mr. Morgan, where's the fire?"

"The fire's *out*," he bellowed, and they almost bore the Rolls to the ground riding the running boards. "Call yourselves firemen? Wait for you characters and we'd not have a stick standing. Young Perry here and I, we put it out, didn't we, boy?"

The *way* he talked to them! To the *Fire* Brigade!

"But see what we have here, you characters. Here, switch the light on there, Denis Benson. At your left hand there. Now what do you characters think of that? Born not twenty minutes ago. Just look at that. Wind your windows down, you Bensons. Don't be shy. Let them get their heads in."

"Gee, ay," the brigade captain said, "that's terrific. Twenty minutes, ay. Doesn't seem possible, you know."

"Isn't that something?" Mr. Morgan boomed. "Brought it into the world himself he did, aided and abetted by his own upstanding son, by young Perry Benson here."

"Split me," the lieutenant said.

Perry was getting patted on the head and Dad was going all coy, still trying to make out it was nothing. Beaming faces, like sunflowers, blossomed at the windows.

"Clears his own block of land," Mr. Morgan boomed, "with the ax and the wrench, no bulldozers for him. Builds his own house of timbers milled from his own logs. Delivers his own daughter. Real, basic manhood, I reckon."

"Split me," the lieutenant said.

"I dips me lid," Mr. Morgan boomed, "even if he is a radical. And she's calling it Denise, as it's right and proper that she should."

"Gee, ay, Mr. Benson. Congratulations. That's terrific."

"If you've got to do it," Dad said, "you've got to

do it. You fellows know that. Take a fire in the middle of the night. If it's there you've got to put it out."

"True, Mr. Benson, that's true. But where was it, so help me? I've got my report to fill in. We've been hunting all over the place. It was lighting up the clouds; that's what he said."

"Who said?" Mr. Morgan boomed.

"The nightman said."

"Bless me heart and soul. He'd say anything to get away from the smell. You don't take any notice of what the nightman says."

"You do when he rings at three-forty A.M. Out near your place somewhere he said. I thought it'd be your incubator room again. Last time, remember? Fifty dozen eggs fried in the shell."

"And we'd have had a lot less if you'd stopped home in bed. You and all your playmates whooping in and out. Scaring me layers out of their wits. Putting them into a molt. The Bensons' chimney it was, going like a bomb. Baby being born, chimney going like a bomb. But young Perry here and I, we sat on it, didn't we, boy? So we'll be seeing you characters again. If you'll pull your heads back and let us get on with the job! Can't waste time yarning with a bunch of nongs who take notice of what the nightman says."

Goodness, he was a terrible man. Perry didn't know where to look. You'd have thought they'd have punched him on the head but their grinning captain shouted back, "Good luck, Mr. Benson. What odds the doctor still sends you the bill?"

Inside light going out, windows winding up, and Mr. Morgan had the Rolls moving again, running on, and Mum was saying, "They're nice men. And it can't be much fun being pulled out in the middle of the night."

But Dad was grumbling, "That doctor had better not send me the bill, he'd better not."

"And they do it all for nothing," Mum said.

"Do it for *nothing*?" exploded Dad. "Touch your hat to them in the street and they charge you for the consultation."

"I'm talking about the Fire Brigade, Denis."

"Well, that's not very kind of you. Splendid voluntary body of men. All this way in the middle of the night and never taking a penny for it. Your attitude astonishes me."

Running on past the track that went down to Walter Piper's house.

"They've got the mumps down there," Perry said. "Imagine Walter being sound asleep in the dark and not knowing anything about it."

"If he's got the mumps he must know," Dad said.

"No argument. If you've got them you've got them. It stands to reason, son."

"It does at that," said Mr. Morgan, "and if I were you I'd take your father's word for it."

Slapping through the potholes full of glistening water, mud showering on the windshield.

"Dum-te-dum-te-dum-te-dum."

Winding through the curves, climbing into the township. There was Perry's school with night lights shining. No one in the classrooms. No one in the playgrounds. Puddles everywhere. Cat's eyes in the grass flashing strangely. Was a fellow awake? Could he be certain?

Steaming down Main Street, tires singing on wet bitumen, shop windows flaking off on either side, the nose of the Rolls getting longer and longer, the speedo reading forty, the speedo reading fifty.

Brrrrrrrrrr.

She was really roaring.

"Whoah," boomed Mr. Morgan.

Leaning back from the wheel stopping a team of horses. Legs out straight flattening the pedals. Dad yelling, "Have you got a puncture?"

"Just passed old Henry. Didn't you see him? On his way to market. Coming out his gate with a load of carrots. Got to tell old Henry. Got to show him. Bless me heart and soul, he'd never forgive me."

Everybody winding down the windows and switching on the lights again, Mr. Morgan sticking his head out as the truck pulled up behind him. "Hey there, Henry Barker. Do you hear me?"

"Is that you, Clarrie Morgan, holding up the traffic? Get your heap off the road or I'll plow through the middle of it. I'm late enough already."

"We've got a baby here, Henry Barker, a brand spanking new one. Not fifteen minutes out of nowhere. Delivered by her father with my assistance."

"A baby *what*, Clarrie Morgan?"

"A baby human."

Slam went the truck door and a head poked in the window: Henry Barker, President of the Football Club, Secretary of the Cricket Club, Treasurer of the Bowling Club, and a preacher on Sundays. "Ah, of course, the Bensons. The loners who do everything the hard way."

"That's us," said Dad with an arm around Mum who was blushing warmly. Nice to see some color in her cheeks again. She had been looking peculiar.

"Born fifteen minutes ago," said Henry Barker, "isn't that remarkable? And what are you, little chicken, a pullet or a rooster?"

"Denise her name is," boomed Mr. Morgan, "after her father, and I'll be asking you, old man, to show some more respect for her."

"Itchy kitchy coo," said Henry Barker, poking out a finger and wrinkling up his features. "When Clarrie can assist at the birth of such a beautiful infant I feel I must remind him that the groundwork God puts in is considerable. Don't forget to bring her in for christening, Mrs. Benson, and buy her a cot cover with my compliments if she hasn't already got one. And God forgive you, Clarrie Morgan, for all the things you lately need forgiving for and I'll bet that's plenty. And who is it you've got beside you? Is that the sixth-grader who took five wickets for thirteen runs against Emerald State School last season? We're keeping an eye on you, young man, and waiting till you're old enough to join the cricket club. What's it like to be a champion fast bowler?"

Roaring on in the Rolls again, the nose getting longer again, forty on the speedo, swooping down through the gullies at the fringe of the forest. "A twenty dollar note," Mum said, "is too much money for that sweet old man to give to relative strangers, even if he can afford it."

Mr. Perry Benson Esquire, Champion Cricketer.

Playing for Australia. Bowling out the Englishmen. See them throwing away their wickets, not game to stand up to him. See them fleeing back to the pavilion, one man after the other, all yelling for their mummies, "Waaahhhh. He's a demon, he's a demon, he's the fastest bowler ever."

"Dum-te-dum-te-dum-te-dum."

Mr. Morgan's tune wasn't getting better. It was worse. If you were going on seventy-one weren't you old enough to know that you sang like a bullfrog? And if you weren't old enough by then how old would you have to be before you did know? And what a terrible fibber! Hadn't his mother ever told him?

Was that a milk cart coming up ahead, all gleaming blue and white? Blue crates and white bottles. Everything sparkling. What a sight. Mr. Morgan giving it a blast on the horn. "Hey there, Milkie," he boomed, roaring past. "Good morning to you."

Fancy being a milkie living in the dark.

White posts with red reflectors flashing past. Fifty on the speedo. Buzzing and purring. Tires zinging in the wet. A man in short pants and red jumper on a pushbike, pushing hard uphill. What was he? A nut? Riding in a race in the middle of the night all by himself? Mr. Morgan giving him a toot. "Hey there, mate."

Front gates and plate glass windows peeling past. Taxi at a No Parking sign, driver sound asleep. Man in black with a big dog on a leash walking from shop to shop. What was he looking for? Two sinister characters with sacks on their backs outside the Methodist Church, real suspicious-looking types, thumbing for a ride.

Robbers going home from work?

"Sorry, mates," Mr. Morgan yelled. "Full up."

Thank goodness for that.

Zoom, zoom, zoom. Zipping past locked-up cars standing at the curb. Where were the people who owned them? Fancy leaving their property outside to get rained on all night with robbers prowling about. Perry turning his head to check on Mum and Dad. So quiet back there he feared they might have vanished. Straining his eyes. Shoulder to shoulder they were, head to head, rocking together from side to side, looking kind of sleepy and kind of nice.

That was a telephone box shining in the dark. Did telephone boxes shine in the day? You'd never know, would you? Someone inside was calling a number. Calling the doctor? Calling the taxi? Was there a lady home at his house having a baby? Or was he calling the Fire Brigade?

There was a van with the tailboard down unloading at a paper shop. There was a man in overalls stacking bundles out of the wet. Bundles of news in black and white. Things that had happened all over the world but people didn't care because they hadn't read it yet. Would there be anything about Mum and Dad, or Perry in the dark, or Mr. Morgan driving his Rolls? All those people snoring their heads off behind drawn blinds, not caring. Perry outside roaring by.

Brrrrrrrr.

Hey, ease up, Mr. Morgan. That's sixty on the speedo. Hey, what you trying to do?

Roaring down the hill from Upwey into Fern Tree Gully. Watch the curve there, Mr. Morgan. Hey, hey, don't swing out so far. Driving at this speed, you silly man, you'll have us in the cutting fighting with the train. Gee willikens, and look at that train go. He must be going as fast as you. He'll be shooting through the station and a mile down the line. Just look at him go, all lit up like a railway train. What else could he look like? I ask you. Whooosshh. Out of the cutting bursting free. Out of the mountains and onto the plain. Is that the first for today or the last for yesterday? But half the questions a fellow might ask he never gets round to saying aloud. Now where have we gone? Street lights shining in layers and levels, like a crowd. Enough light shining around here to last in our house for years and years. Could a fellow stuff some in his schoolbag and take it home? They'd never miss it, would they? "Cast your eyes on this, Mum," he'd say. "Light to last for donkey's years. Got it in me schoolbag. But how do we let a little out so that the rest doesn't get away?"

What are we stopping for?

"Gee, Mr. Morgan! *Is this the hospital?* Are we there?"

"Now, you people, stay as you are. Stay in the warm. I'll be back in the shake of a wee lamb's tail as soon as I know what you have to do."

Crack went the door and off went the man looking so huge and the Rolls seemed to sigh and take a breath of air and raise itself an inch or two.

"Isn't he a dear," Mum said, "but haven't I been saying it for years? That if we gave him half a chance. . . . Denis, you've despised that man. . . ."

Dad made a noise that wasn't a word, maybe a grunt or a yawn. "Don't go to sleep, dear," Mum said. "Wake up, Denis. You mustn't give in. You've been marvelous until now." Perry could have sworn that he heard a slapping sound.

"All right," Dad said, but his voice was slurred as if he had become very tired. "Sure, sure," said Dad after a while, "I reckon I'll buy two. We could do with a spare."

Out of the hospital doors came people in line, sisters in white and nurses in blue, one after the other swinging their arms, gee willikens, it was like something you saw on the screen. Sisters and nurses and wheel-chairs and Mr. Morgan, too. Like a great wave sweeping up and over, breaking over the Rolls, swamping the place with legs and arms and *oohs* and *aahs* as if they had never seen a baby before. Drowning Perry in people.

Swimming up to the surface and finding a great calm. A great silence. A great aloneness.

Gee. . . . And I don't even know the time. Where've they all gone? Going off and leaving me. I hope those robbers don't come by. I'm nobody, I am. I'm the fellow that gets left behind. I'm the fellow that gets shut outside. No one knows that I'm around. . . .

I'm not going to get a look-in now. Blooming baby. Have you ever seen anything so strange? I don't reckon it's a baby at all. All the babies I've seen before had faces. . . .

Leaving me out here. I'll betcha they're in there having cream cakes. I'll betcha they're in there having a wonderful time. . . .

Sitting up suddenly, senses scattered, wildly alarmed, something had changed.

"You're awake. I won't have to carry you now."

Mr. Morgan was looking him in the eye. Mr. Morgan with sunlight on his face.

"All right, boy. We're home. Get down."

Get down, he said. That's what he said. Get down from the Rolls. Get down and out and onto the ground and wake from the dream. That ground down there was the end of the dream. He'd fall through it as he'd fall through a cloud and wake up at home in bed. But the ground was hard.

"Are you sick, boy?"

Perry shook his head.

"You've been asleep for hours. With your mouth wide open!"

It was real. It was real.

"How does it feel to be a big brother now?"

Perry thought about that. Stood there thinking about it. He liked the sound of it. "Good."

"I've brought you home to my place. Your Dad's head, you know, the injury. They're keeping him in for a day or two. He's all right, you're not to worry. But his head is very sore. He's not well enough yet to look after you."

Walking through the sunshine to Mr. Morgan's door.

"Do you want to sleep?"

"Oh, no."

"Like some breakfast now?"

"Yes, please."

"Omelette? With cheese and onion and herbs?"

"Oh, yes, please."

"What about school? Do you want to go today?"

"The kids, they won't believe it, will they?"

He was a giant all right. He was huge. But someone had chopped the beanstalk down. *Traps set. Baits laid.* I wonder why he can be so kind but yet so cruel?

Inside the door, that cold white room where Perry had stood in a puddle with water ringing him round. Something stopped him as he went stepping through. Something warm. There was sunshine on the walls and sunshine on the floor and in that ink-stained desk a deep red friendly glow, even if the apple core did look properly chewed.